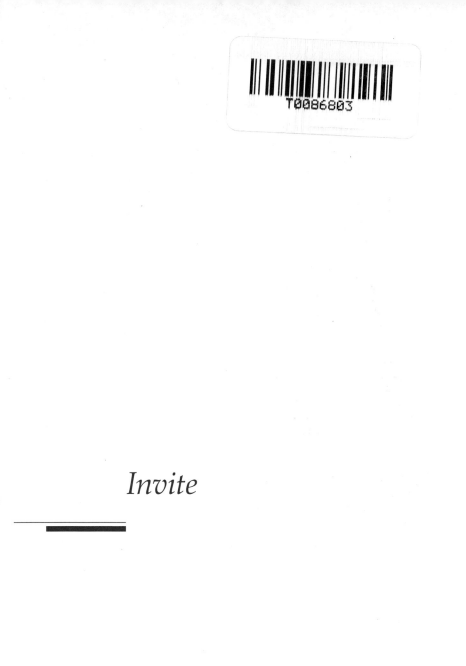

Invite

The

Iowa

Short

Fiction

Award

In honor of
James O. Freedman

Grateful acknowledgment
to John A. Crawford for
supporting the publication
of this book

University of

Iowa Press

Iowa City

*Glen
Pourciau*

Invite

University of Iowa Press, Iowa City 52242

Copyright © 2008 by Glen Pourciau

www.uiowapress.org

Printed in the United States of America

The University of Iowa Press is a member of Green Press
Initiative and is committed to preserving natural resources.
Printed on acid-free paper

Library of Congress Cataloging-in-Publication Data

Pourciau, Glen, 1951–

   Invite / Glen Pourciau.

      p.   cm.—(Iowa short fiction award)

   Short stories.

   ISBN-13: 978-1-58729-692-5 (pbk.)

   ISBN-10: 1-58729-692-6 (pbk.)

   I. Title.

   PS3616.O86816 2008   2008010761

   813'.6—dc22

08   09   10   11   12   P   5   4   3   2   1

For my wife, Linda,

Always

Contents

ACKNOWLEDGMENTS

The stories in this collection were first published in the following magazines: "Snub," "Among the Missing," "How Tommy Lee Turned Out Abnormal," and "Deep Wilderness" in the *New England Review*; "Gone" and "The Neighbor" in the *Ontario Review*; "Water" and "The Dangerous Couple" in the *Mississippi Review*; and "Shake" in the *New Orleans Review*.

I am grateful to Stephen Donadio, editor of the *New England Review*, for his ongoing support of my stories over a number of years. You helped my fingers move on the keys. Thanks also to Raymond Smith at the *Ontario Review*, Frederick Barthelme at the *Mississippi Review*, and Christopher Chambers at the *New Orleans Review* for publishing stories in this collection.

Most of all, thank you, Linda, for taking the long trip with me.

Invite

Snub

The trouble started when my wife and I were planning a trip to see friends in a town where we once lived. As we talked about who we wanted to see and what we wanted to do, we decided we didn't want to see a couple we knew there named the Crossmans. He was a relentless talker who repeated the same stories over and over. His stories often involved a perceived injustice done to him by people he saw as unreasonable and uncomprehending. The Crossmans' dog was a nuisance, and it was nearly always with them. Wherever it was, it yapped constantly, and they seemed not to care about the noise and would let it go on barking at will. They took it with them to dog-friendly restaurants, where it sat perched on Mrs. Crossman's lap, and when it took a break from yapping they amused themselves by talking baby talk to it. Another reason we didn't want to be around them was that they were both nonstop smokers and drinkers. After every puff of her cigarette she exhaled long streams of smoke as if she had a fire burning in her lungs. She was famous for taking falls while drunk, especially going down steps, and she broke an arm, a leg, an ankle, or a collarbone whenever she fell. She started walking with a cane to help her keep her balance. As we listened to them over the course of several years we began to notice a lack of awareness of us. We wondered if they'd be saying exactly the same things if someone else were sitting in front of them. With these thoughts in mind, I suggested that we skip the Crossmans. Don't call them, don't let them know we're around. We agreed to this plan, though they'd always treated us as friends. They'd had us over for dinner to meet their son when he was in town and had invited us to their parties. I'd played golf with him more than a dozen times.

We were on the last day of our trip, seated at the far end of the patio of a popular restaurant, looking over our menus, when the Crossmans came in and sat at a table on the other end of the patio. Mrs. Crossman propped her cane against a chair, holding the lap dog in her free hand, and sat facing us, while he sat with his back to us. There were several occupied tables between our table and theirs, but at times, she had a clear view of my face, depending on which way the people between our tables were leaning. We had to decide whether to get up and say hello or try to stick it out and hope they didn't see us. We chose to stick it out, and if they caught us we planned to pretend we hadn't seen them. We worried they wouldn't be convinced by the lie, and we also worried they'd sit there and drink for hours and still be at their table when we got up to leave. Their dog was in an outgoing mood, yapping, craning its jittery neck from side to side, probably frustrated that it couldn't take a drag from her cigarette. All during the meal we talked about our escape. Near our table there were steps that led up into the restaurant. We could reach the steps quickly and go inside, but the wall on that side was all glass. We'd have to pass the Crossmans' table, and if they turned their heads they could see us through the glass. She'd be the one with the best view, but if he noticed movement he might turn and see us.

We paid the bill and waited for a moment when they'd be distracted. When she leaned over to look for something in her purse we made our move. We pushed our chairs back and started for the steps, not looking in their direction. I opened the door and we went inside, keeping our backs to the Crossmans as much as we could. We then moved ahead, and as we approached the place where we were nearest to them, I felt completely naked. She'd already finished digging in her purse and was sitting upright, puffing a cigarette, surrounded by a cloud of smoke, and she turned her head toward us as we went by. She glanced at us for a moment, but her face did not change expression. She said nothing to Crossman, and his head did not turn.

As soon as we turned away from them my wife said she wanted to go to the bathroom. I asked her not to. She said she needed to go. I said that if one of the Crossmans went to the bathroom it would be impossible for them not to see us. We'd have to act as if we didn't know they were there. We'd end up going back to their table and listening to his stories—how he met her famous father, how intimidated he was, how he'd told his jerk of a boss that he was retiring at the age of fifty and that the boss had said he couldn't possibly retire, he was too young. He'd tell us who was angry at him and who had been angry at him and that he'd never said or done whatever they claimed he'd said or done. On and on, with the dog carrying on in our ears, trying to be heard over Crossman. And that would be if things went well, if they weren't offended that we'd sat through a whole meal avoiding them. I said it would be better for her to wait for another bathroom. I didn't want to stand and wait for her alone in such a vulnerable position. She told me to wait outside, she had to go right now. I asked her what she'd say if Mrs. Crossman came in the bathroom and saw her or if she came out of the bathroom and found herself face to face with Mr. Crossman. She'd have to go outside and tell me to come back in because the Crossmans would like us to join them. She gave in, and we left. As we looked for another bathroom, we wondered if Mrs. Crossman had seen us when we walked by their table and what she would have said if she had.

Six months later my wife returned for a visit alone. She stayed with a friend of hers who'd remained close and whose husband was out of town for a week. The friend wanted company and her husband's trip was a chance for them to spend some time together. They'd met two other women for lunch at the same restaurant where we'd seen the Crossmans and as they were eating, my wife heard yapping and looked up and saw the Crossmans walking in with their dog. One of the women at my wife's table waved at them, and they immediately came over to say hello to her. My wife said hello when they made eye contact, but they seemed not to know who she was. When she and her friends left the restaurant, they stopped by the Crossmans' table. Again the Crossmans looked at her without recognition, and she, not knowing what she should do, did not identify herself.

She phoned that night and told me what had happened. I asked her what she made of it and she said she didn't know what to make of it. Maybe they didn't recognize her because she wasn't with me or because they were too drunk to see clearly. She couldn't tell how drunk they were, she said, they seemed the way they always did. She'd asked her friend if she thought they knew who she was, and her friend said that she'd met Crossman half a dozen times before she could tell she seemed familiar to him but that Mrs. Crossman had never had any trouble remembering her. My wife pointed out that her situation was different. They already knew her and it was a question of whether they could have both forgotten her. I asked if she thought they could be paying us back for the snub. Mrs. Crossman had probably seen us walk by their table, I said. My wife answered that even though Mrs. Crossman had turned her head toward us, she may not have registered who we were. She wasn't expecting to see us. We might have seemed somewhat familiar to her, but we were out of her field of vision quickly. She may have turned back to her drink and never given us another thought. Still, my wife wasn't sure they hadn't known her, despite the blank looks she'd seen on their faces.

I kept thinking about it after talking to her. Crossman's temper was legendary. Some people refused to play golf with him because of his outbursts when he hit a bad shot. I'd seen him bash a five iron against a tree until the shaft split, and there was the well-known story of the day he hit a ball in a pond and reacted by throwing most of his clubs in the water after it. Then it occurred to him that he needed the clubs to finish the round so he jumped in the pond and fished them out. He played the last six holes soaking wet, complaining the whole time about how filthy the pond was. I remembered seeing his anger come out in his stories of the injustices done to him, and the more I thought about it the more it made sense to me that the Crossmans could be getting even with us.

A few weeks after my wife returned she got a call from the friend she'd stayed with. She'd run into the Crossmans again, and apparently out of the blue, they'd asked if she'd heard from us recently and if she knew how we were doing. She told the Crossmans that my wife had just been there and that they'd seen her at the restaurant. They seemed surprised to hear it and wondered why she hadn't said anything to them and why she hadn't called them and suggested getting together. Her friend knew the story of the afternoon we'd avoided the Crossmans, and she feared they might be looking for a reaction to their questions. She didn't address their questions but told the Crossmans that she'd let us know they'd asked about us. Crossman then said he'd give us a call to check in and asked her to tell us that he'd be in touch.

When I got home from work that evening my wife told me right away about her friend's call. I told her I couldn't believe that what the Crossmans had said to her friend was a coincidence. They must know we'd snubbed them, and they'd done the same to her in return, pretending they didn't remember who she was. Crossman was now going to call and put us in the awkward position of covering up the snub, though we could guess that he probably already knew about it. He wanted us to squirm for what we'd done. My wife said that maybe he just wanted to see how we were doing. I admitted it was possible, but it was just that possibility that would allow him to play the role he could be playing. We wanted to ignore them, so Crossman was going to stick himself right in our faces. I asked her how likely it seemed that the Crossmans would ask about us so soon after they seemed not to recognize her at the restaurant. She answered that perhaps her image was familiar to one of them and that at a subconscious level it recalled a memory of us. I couldn't deny that her explanation could be true. I couldn't let myself go wholeheartedly into the darkness I suspected Crossman of creating, but his behavior fit the pattern of the angry man I knew. I could imagine him raging to his wife about our ingratitude and thinking of a scheme to make us pay for turning up our noses at their friendship.

Sure enough, Crossman called. I heard his voice on the recorder and picked it up without a pause. He was all charm, more so than I ever remembered. They missed seeing us and talking to us, he said, and he just wanted to see how we were doing; they really wanted to know. They'd love it if we'd drop them a note from time to time to let them know what we were up to. I started off friendly, not saying anything to suggest the undercurrent of tension I felt. Then Crossman brought up the subject of running into my wife at the restaurant with her group of friends. He and his wife had discussed it and they wondered why she wouldn't have said anything to them. It hurt their feelings, he told me, that she'd passed them by without any personal acknowledgment or sense of familiarity. When they heard it had been her standing in front of them, they felt embarrassed they hadn't recognized her and decided it was up to them to apologize. They'd been planning to phone us and catch up anyway. He asked if my wife had felt embarrassed that they didn't seem to know her and if that was why she hadn't spoken to them. I said I didn't know the answer to that question and asked Crossman why they hadn't spoken to her. Crossman ignored my implication that they may have been pretending not to remember her. He was concerned that we were offended they hadn't remembered her, and he explained that between age and booze their memories were getting worse every day. They hadn't forgotten us, he said, and in fact, they talked about us quite often. One thing they said was that they never saw us anymore. Then he asked me how long it had been since I'd paid the town a visit. Was he setting me up for a confrontation? Would he throw the lie in my face if I denied we'd been in town at the time of the snub? I told him the truth about the last time we'd been there. Why didn't you call us up, at least, and say hello? he asked. We could have gotten together for lunch, he said, and then named the restaurant where we'd seen them. I added up the coincidences. I didn't like being put in this position and I told him so. He said he didn't know what I meant. What position? he asked. I felt an urge to bring it all out into the open, to admit we'd snubbed them and to accuse them of knowing it. But he could deny everything and make me look like a fool. For some reason I remembered a time he drove me home after a round of golf. We'd stopped somewhere for a few beers on the way back, and it was dark when he stopped to let me out in front of the house.

As I walked toward my front door, Crossman also got out of his car and went around to the back of it. I turned to see what he was doing. I saw him unzip his pants, pull out his penis, and let a thick stream of urine flow onto the street. I took a second look to make sure I wasn't imagining it, but there was Crossman, shaking off the last drops and putting his penis back in his pants.

I then told Crossman that I thought he'd known who my wife was when he saw her at the restaurant and that he'd intentionally snubbed her. The words jumped straight out of my mouth. He paused and I heard him gulp something down. He asked me why in the world he would do that. We'd been friends for years and he'd have no reason to snub her. She'd always been delightful to them. I told him I found it hard to believe that as many times as we'd been together he could forget my wife and not know when he was face to face with her in broad daylight. Crossman said that he could tell I was offended and he again apologized for their memory lapse, but he wanted me to understand that he would never make a conscious effort to snub me or my wife in a public place, especially not in front of our friends. He asked me to take his word on that. I told him I had a hard time accepting his version of what happened. Crossman then said he was sorry the conversation wasn't going as he'd hoped it would. He had the feeling that I didn't want to talk with him, and he regretted knowing that. He asked me to be sure to pass along their apologies. He wished us the best and hung up.

My wife had been listening to me and I filled her in on what Crossman had said. She thought I should call him back and apologize. I didn't know if any of the things I was thinking about him were true, she said, and the Crossmans had never been anything but good to us. Too many coincidences, I said. They're probably just trying to keep in touch with us, she answered. Maybe, I said. Maybe is enough, she said, because you have no reason to assume the worst about them. I agreed that she could be right, but I didn't call back. I told her that Crossman could be manipulating me, waiting for me to call and make some groveling attempt to get him to forgive me. Then he could laugh in my face and ask me if I wanted to apologize for snubbing them in the first place. He could repeat the story all over town, congratulating himself on his success in paying me back.

As I tried to sleep that night I kept going over the whole scenario, nagged by the fear that I was being unfair to the Crossmans. My wife lay awake next to me, her chest heaving with the effort not to start an argument. As the first light entered the bedroom I told her that I'd decided to call Crossman and apologize, that I'd risk exposure to humiliation rather than live in the world of suspicion and bitterness I'd churned up in myself.

Later that morning I called him and said I'd overreacted when I'd talked to him the day before. It was off base, I said, for me to assume that they'd purposely ignored my wife. I'd worked myself into a mental state, and my anger had taken over and created an absurd nightmare of an interpretation. I said I hoped he would accept my apology. Crossman seemed to be sniveling as he listened to what I said. He thanked me for the explanation and abruptly ended the call.

I put down the phone, still unsure what to think of him. Was he pulling the strings, leading me into a pit of shame? Were he and his wife sitting out on their patio with drinks, deciding what they'd do next?

Mrs. Crossman called the following night and spoke to my wife. Crossman was devastated, she said, by the way I'd reacted to his phone call. She wanted to make contact and add her apology for all the unpleasantness. She added that not acknowledging someone can have many unforeseen consequences and that she wished she'd said something to my wife when they'd seen her at the restaurant. My wife asked if she was saying that she had recognized her. Mrs. Crossman hesitated and then admitted that she had thought it was her, but she'd told herself she must be mistaken since my wife hadn't spoken to them. She asked my wife why she hadn't said anything to them when she'd obviously known who they were. My wife said that they didn't seem to know her and it would have embarrassed her to remind them in front of her friends. Mrs. Crossman said she thought it would have been just as embarrassing that the Crossmans didn't seem to know her. My wife said she had been embarrassed by that. Mrs. Crossman then assured my wife that she would never intentionally ignore her.

I was sitting in front of the TV with the mute on as they talked. After the call, my wife sat next to me on the couch and gave me the rundown. I could see that Mrs. Crossman had gotten her thinking. Maybe they did see us that day, she said.

Two nights later, Crossman phoned again. My wife answered and he gave her a friendly greeting and asked to speak with me. Crossman told me that he was sorry about all the unfortunate misunderstandings and he wanted to make up with us. He said he understood anger, he'd been angry at people himself and there had been times when he struggled to keep it from taking over all of his waking thoughts. He could remember many occasions, he said, when he'd been angry at someone and thought that something about them was true while at the same time wondering if it really was true. He could see how my mind would run away with itself, fueled by the anger I felt. There had been days and nights when he wanted to grab people by the neck and tear their heads off, and he realized when he got to that point he had to get a grip on himself and rise above his anger. The world was not a perfect place. He didn't want me to think he had any ill feelings toward me, no matter what had happened. He hoped that we could still be friends and get together when we visited. They'd love to see us.

I didn't know what to answer. I could have told Crossman that I knew what he was up to, but I didn't know. I imagined him laughing at me on the other end, sensing my struggle as I read between the lines. I heard the dog yapping behind him somewhere. My anger choked me. I couldn't get a word out, and no words came to mind.

Among
the
Missing

"My wife and I never recovered from the loss of
our son," my dinner guest began after swallowing his last bite of
food and wiping his mouth for the last time. Dinner had been on
the table when he arrived because I knew he would be hungry. He
had almost no money and was too inept to prepare himself a decent meal. Why I wanted to help him eat I did not understand, but
throughout my adult life I had occasionally invited him over for
dinner. Even before that, when we were children and schoolmates,
I had listened to him and taken an interest in his well-being. But
there was a price to pay, and the price was that I had to listen to
what he said, and once he started he would not stop talking. It was
always after dinner that he began, and after all the years I had

known him he never tired of telling me his personal history, if you could call it that. While eating he concentrated on his food; he gave himself totally to it, at times groaning with pleasure as he ate. And when he was finished on this visit he cleared his throat and coughed, leaned on his elbows and pushed his empty plate forward so that it would not interfere with his arms and hands. "It was the suddenness of it, the unexpectedness that burdened us more than anything. It was the failure to ever be able to answer the mystery. Instead we were left only with questions, fantastic scenarios to fill our minds with, to talk endlessly about with no hope of knowing the truth of what had happened to him. He was a strange boy, driven to unusual behavior by forces within him that we had no idea how to interpret. My wife, now my ex-wife, believed that my talking, the constant flow of words that I subjected him to, had something to do with his problems. But often he would seek me out when I was alone and would sit at my side and wait for me to speak. If I was talking to his mother he would hide around a corner so that he could hear what I was saying. Why would he do those things if he was disturbed by the sound of my voice or by the stories I told him? My wife could not answer this question, except to say that he was interested in me because I was his father. And though he wanted to hear what I would say, she said, he may still have been driven away by what I had already said and by a conflicting fear or dread of listening to me in the future. She became obsessed by the idea that my voice was inside the boy and that it was related in some way to his behavior, though he was not acting out any specific situation I had described or doing anything I said I'd done. Neither of us could make any specific connection between what I said and what he did. Neither of us could explain why he kept entering other people's houses or why he stayed there so long once he was inside. His entries seemed harmless in a way. He never forced a door open or broke a window, never stole anything, and never destroyed any property. When people returned from work or vacation or from the mall or the grocery store they might find him there, taking a nap on one of their beds or eating a bowl of cereal at the kitchen table or feeding and talking to a pet. He would greet them and sometimes even start a conversation with them as if everything were normal, asking if they'd had a good trip or a good day. People called us during the day and at night to say that our son was in their house acting as if he lived there, and we were on the one hand relieved to know where he'd been for the last several hours or more and on the other hand embarrassed and at a loss for an explanation. Sometimes we knew the people who called us about our son and other times strangers who lived several blocks away called after asking him for his phone number. He was not old enough when this behavior started to be threatening to most people, though some people got hysterical at the sight of him. Some people immediately phoned the police and said that a young intruder was watching their television or whatever. Some of the people who knew us refused to talk to me if I answered the phone. They would sigh at the sound of my voice, fearing a lengthy conversation, and ask to speak to my wife. If I went on talking they might hang up and call back until my wife answered. It was an awkward situation for everyone concerned. We took him to psychologists, who at first wanted all of us to attend therapy sessions, but after listening to me go on and on, they began to focus solely on our son. But none of these sessions seemed to help, and the behavior never stopped until he left. The day he disappeared we had no way of knowing that he was gone for good. We thought his absence signaled another intrusion and that he would probably return before bedtime, but when he didn't show up all that night we knew that something was different. We called the owners of some of his favorite houses and asked if they had seen him or if they had heard any word of his whereabouts, but no one had any idea where he was. We never heard another word from him and neither of us has heard a single sound from him since the day he left. We wondered if he'd met a bad end, if someone had come home into a house he'd entered and pulled a gun and shot him on sight. They could have thrown him in the trunk of their car and driven away with him and dumped his body in a place where no one could ever find it or identify it. We wondered if he'd left because something snapped in his mind that caused him to take a turn for the worse. He had been quiet during the time before he left and he had been through bouts with nightmares and sleepwalking. He began getting in my car while he was asleep and driving all over town in his underwear, which he always slept in. One night he returned home in the middle of the night, though we never knew that he'd left, stumbled through the door connecting the house to the garage, and fell down on the floor, moaning and muttering. We heard him thump when he landed and heard him carrying on and we jumped out of bed to see what sort of hell had broken loose. He'd been in a fight with a gang of drunks, he told us, and he hadn't woken up until his face was being smashed in. His face was swollen and bruised and bleeding, and his knees were scuffed up and his ribs sore. He was wearing nothing but a pair of ripped briefs and according to him the guys had just come out of a bar and had jumped him because they didn't like the way he was dressed. But even when he slept at home in his bed, some nights were peculiar, owing to his habit of carrying on long conversations with imaginary people in his sleep. We would go to his doorway and switch on his light when we heard the racket, and this was not enough to wake him up, though he often answered us when we spoke to him as if we were part of his dream. Our son had become increasingly unpredictable, which made us fret all the more about his fate when he disappeared. We could imagine dozens of ways that he could hurt himself or be hurt, and we could hardly imagine any way that he could take care of himself in a normal manner and come out all right. The police could not find him, and the detectives we hired could find no trace of him. We read books on how to search for people, but no matter what method or trick we used, there was no sign of our son anywhere in the world. After a while we even hoped that he'd entered someone's house and been taken in as family, protected and nurtured by someone with his interests at heart. And always, after he left, he was between us and in everything we did. Our marriage was doomed, but even after separating and then divorcing we could not leave our son behind and we could not turn ourselves around and start over from the point where things had gone wrong. Sometimes I get a call and no one is on the other end of the line and I wonder if it is him. The caller often stays on the line and listens and waits for me to say something and other times puts the phone down as soon as I pick it up. I start thinking about him then and ask myself all over again where he could be and what could have happened to him. I cannot stop thinking about him and I have on a few occasions called my wife, but when she hears my voice she immediately hangs up on me. I have written to her but she will not answer my letters, and I suspect that she does not even read them before she rips them to shreds and throws them away or burns them. I admit they are long letters, but I cannot write a short letter on this subject. And even though she will not talk to me when I call or write back to me when I write, and even though we are divorced, it is still better knowing where she is than not knowing, to have some tenuous connection with my former life. Though all that part of my life is over it is not over, it is everything to me, it is everywhere inside me, it is in the taste of my food, in my breath, and of course in my voice. "Wake up!" he shouted suddenly and banged his knife on his plate. I had closed my eyes for a moment and they had closed several other times, but each time I'd snapped them open. "I know you've heard this story before," he said, "but I'd rather not tell it while you're sleeping." He was right, I had heard the story before, and because I knew him I also knew that he had never been married and had never had a son. But whenever I'd pointed this out to him in the past, he would stare at me and then go on as if I'd said nothing, and so I'd given up interrupting him. "I know you don't believe me," he said, and it was the first time he had ever said this to me. "The story is true," he went on, "but in reality I am not the father but the missing son. I left my parents when I was sixteen and I have never been back to see them even once. I have never watched them from a distance, but I have checked phone directories for their names and that is how I know they got divorced. I am the son who entered the houses of strangers and fed their pets and slept in their beds. Why did I leave? I do not know, even after years of puzzling over the question. All I can say is that I wanted to be somewhere else, which is why I kept attempting to live in other people's houses and why I rose in my sleep and set out in my father's car without knowing where I was going or that I was going at all. I left a note for my parents explaining why I was leaving, despite the fact that I did not know why. Yet I left them some explanation, which I am sure made no sense to them, and I packed up and left while they were both at work one day. I asked that they not attempt to search for me, that they accept the fact that if they got me back I would only leave again. My mother must have been happy to see me go since my father was also a talker, and one talker in a household is more than enough. She was forced to listen to both of us; there was no letup, and I cannot remember any word my mother ever spoke to me and can only vaguely remember the sound of her voice. I suspect they both may have been secretly relieved I left them because as far as I know they never made any effort to find me. I have never done anything to hide from them. Wherever I have lived I have had my name listed in the directory. But I didn't blame them for not searching for me; they were at their wits' end trying to keep me out of people's houses and there was no way they could watch me every minute. I must have been looking for something in all those houses, something I didn't find, something that was not there in all the portraits on the walls that I talked to or in all the closets that I stood in looking over the clothes. In some cases I even put on their clothes, which never fit me, and stood in front of the mirror and spoke to myself as if I were the other person speaking to me, though I did not know the other person in any of these cases. I sometimes went on until the people came home, and as I heard them entering I felt in a way that they were intruding on me. I also felt disappointed that I would have to go back home, and I don't know where this feeling came from. There was nothing I could name in any of these houses that was not in the house where I lived, and neither of my parents mistreated me in any way that I can remember. Looking back, this feeling that I did not want to be at home, that I did not feel at home when I was at home, may have started after my dog ran away from me for the last time. I'd had my dog, a collie, for years and I talked to him constantly when we were together. We would lie in the grass in the backyard together or I would sit in a chair on the patio and he would sit or lie at my side and listen to the stories I told him. I told my dog stories that were completely true about my life—about who I'd been talking to, about dreams I'd had and the conversations in those dreams, and about whatever else occurred to me—and I also told my dog stories that most people would have said were completely untrue. But the dog didn't know the difference and I would continue until, after a long while, the dog would go to sleep. And whenever my dog went to sleep I would wake him up immediately, or as soon as I noticed it, and this would usually go on with the dog going to sleep and my waking up the dog until I was interrupted by my mother calling me in for dinner or some such reason. During these long talks I had with my dog he would grumble and groan and sometimes howl as I spoke, but he would stay at my side no matter how uncomfortable and sleepy he became. There were times when I stopped talking just for the sake of the dog, when I sensed that the dog simply could not stand to listen to me any longer. Even when I watched television I would sit with my dog and talk all during the programs we watched. I would talk to the characters in the story and the story itself and the commercials and to my dog about all those things and my dog listened to me, occasionally looking up at me and gazing at my face and particularly my mouth. But then my dog began to run away from home. It was the only way he could escape my voice when he couldn't put up with me anymore. He would disappear and I would search the neighborhood calling his name. The first time he left he was gone for about a week, as I remember it, and then one morning I found him curled up on our front porch when I went out to get the newspaper for my dad. He jumped to his feet when he saw me and lifted his forelegs and put them on my chest and licked my face. I held him and took him inside and fed him and gave him water. He had lost weight and he seemed tense and anxious, glad to be back home. I sat with him almost the whole day telling him how I'd looked for him and how we'd missed him and asking him where he'd been, if he'd left on purpose or if he'd just gotten lost, and I invented stories of his adventures alone and with the other dogs he might have met. For months we went along as before, and then one day he was gone again. The day before, he had been extremely restless as he listened to me, and I'd even cut myself short because he went off into a fury of howling, which made every dog in the neighborhood howl as if they were shouting me down. I couldn't hear myself talk by then anyway so I thought it best to give us both a rest. He wanted to sleep outside that night and I guess he must have jumped the fence, because in the morning he was nowhere to be found. Again I looked for him and again I found nothing. I posted signs on telephone poles and offered a reward, a reward that I did not have the money to pay, but I was desperate. At night I would stand in the yard shouting his name in case he was in the area and couldn't find his way home. And one day he was in the backyard again, pacing on the grass with his head down, as if he were defeated or ashamed. He was thinner than he'd been after the first trip away and he devoured the special meal I made for him out of leftovers. I gave him a day of peace before I spoke to him, but then, fearing that he would think he was being punished, I sat down with him on the floor of my room and told him what had happened since he left. This time he did not stay for long. Less than a week after returning he ran away again and I have never seen him since. The longer I went without seeing him the more convinced I became that he would never return, whether because he did not want to come back or because he'd had some kind of accident that made returning impossible I cannot say. But I was never the same after he left. I had lost my constant companion and listener. My father offered to buy me another dog, but I feared losing the new one and so I turned down his offer. Soon after that I began entering houses, began a process of more involved mental wandering, though my mind had always wandered down many trails. It was during my searches for my dog that I became more familiar with the neighborhood. I would go down the street ringing doorbells, asking if anyone had seen him, in the process becoming aware that certain people were hardly ever at home. I could tell who had an alarm system since those who did put signs in their yards or stickers in their windows to warn off burglars. There was a gulf at home. Neither of my parents wanted to listen to me, my father because he was always talking himself, my mother because she was always listening to my father. I took refuge in the homes of others, perhaps hoping subconsciously that I would find my dog living in one of them. Even now that I am grown I still have the urge to go into houses and look through people's drawers and closets, but I cannot let myself do that anymore, I cannot live that way. I have been lucky in my life to have had other contact with people, to have known people who were willing to listen to me talk, such as you and others, people who in spite of my relentless style of speaking still have me over, even though I never have anyone over and would not know what to do if I did except sit and talk. But despite the listeners I have had there have been many times, I admit, when I could have had more listeners at hand, when I found myself collaring people at the library or on the street at a bus stop or wherever. Some of these complete strangers have been patient with me and willing to listen while others have walked away as soon as I've opened my mouth. In one case I met a couple with more than the usual interest in listening at a party that I believe you attended and that you may even have given, I don't remember. Anyway, this couple and I fell into a long discussion in which I did almost all the talking and several people who knew me stuck their heads in the middle of us as they walked by and told the couple that there was no way of shutting me up and they would not be able to get away from me unless they turned on their heels and ran for their lives, or something like that. The couple laughed at these warnings and they seemed to want me to keep talking, which I was happy to do. After the party they invited me over to their house for a drink, and it was obvious from their clothes and their car and their house that they were rich, or at least they thought they were rich. We sat up all night sipping drinks and I talked to them until the three of us were so sleepy we could hardly hold our heads up. They offered me a bed in a guest room and after we'd slept for a few hours we got up and ate a huge breakfast of steak and eggs. I started up again and they sat there listening to me, not knowing what to make of whatever I was saying but wanting more and more. Finally, one of them got around to asking me what I did for a living and I said not much of anything and they offered to hire me to talk to them. It wasn't fair, they said, to expect me to talk for hours on end and not get anything for my time. I was completely astounded. I couldn't believe that this couple would be willing to pay me to talk, and they even offered to pay me for what I'd already said to them. And for a short time, during the brief period that I collected paychecks from them, I began to feel like a well-adjusted and productive member of society. They paid me daily and by the hour, and for almost a week they listened to every word I said and seemed unable to tear themselves away. Then signs of stress began to appear. The wife began to hold her head and rock herself as I spoke and the husband made noises of his own in order to block out the sound of my words. Sometimes he would jump in on me and shout in my face that I was contradicting something I'd said three days before or make some other objection. Still, they went on listening to me, practically writhing with discomfort, their eyes bulging and weeping. It was painful for me to watch, but I was being paid to do a job, and they hadn't fired me or even told me to stop. But one day the wife stood up from the den sofa, where she was sitting next to her husband, and doubled over and twisted her hands through her hair and started screaming that she wanted me to be quiet, she couldn't endure it for another second. Her husband was so relieved that he let out a mammoth sigh and then delivered a little speech to me, a speech which seemed to drag him up from the sofa. He could not make any sense of what I said anymore, he told me, there was no way that all of it could be true, if any of it was, but the main problem was that he and his wife understood and believed every word I had said, and in the end it was what they understood and believed rather than what they didn't understand and believe that was causing them to send me on my way. He sounded almost apologetic by the end of his speech and without offering any further explanation he fled to his bedroom and closed the door. I was left alone in the den with his wife. After pausing only briefly she approached the cushion where I was sitting and asked me to stand up, and when I did she propositioned me. She whispered her request in my ear and leaned against me as she whispered, her wet lips touching my earlobe. She asked if I would meet her somewhere, she didn't care where it was, but she also asked me to promise that I would not say one word to her. She wanted only silence out of me from now on, and she would scream if I ever told her another story again. I answered that her request was impossible, that I was all talk and that talk was the only thing she would ever get out of me. She held me against her for a moment and then stepped back a few steps and asked me to leave. I started to say something, but she held up her hand and said, 'Please,' and I nodded and backed away from her and left. They mailed me my final check and I have never heard from them again. But I confess that for some time after that I felt an occasional urge to enter their house and walk through it and examine all of their belongings in detail, to sit down on their furniture and look through their photo albums and even cook a meal on their stovetop and use their dishes and flatware to eat it. I never went inside again, but several times I parked my car down the street and sat watching their house. And one morning when I was there I saw her come out around eleven to pick up their newspaper, I assume after sleeping late. I had been wondering if the newspaper could be a sign that the couple was out of town, and as I was resisting an impulse to imagine myself inside their house she emerged from the front door in a white terry cloth robe and walked to the paper holding her robe shut around her throat, even though the robe was tied tight around her waist and it was a warm day and the sun was shining down on her. It was the only time I'd seen her since I left the day of our final discussion, and when she leaned over to pick up her paper she looked down the street and saw my car and then saw me. She straightened up with her paper and stood on the sidewalk staring at me and she did not move for several long moments. I could see that it meant something for her to see me, and even after she turned and started back up the walk she stopped and looked in my direction before going inside. I sat where I was, though I had an edgy feeling that I should be going and wondered if she would tell her husband she had seen me and if he would come charging outside and run toward my car and bang on my window and demand an explanation I did not have. But nothing happened. I waited maybe fifteen minutes and then drove away, and I have never been back. Something about seeing her and her seeing me gave me a sense of completion." He paused, apparently pondering the sense of completion he'd gotten from seeing and being seen by the woman again, if they had seen each other again, if they'd ever seen each other in the first place. I knew that he was not the missing son, that he had never run away from his parents, and that his dog had never run away from home since he'd never had a dog, and so it seemed likely that the couple he'd been talking about had never existed. Yet I sat listening to him. "Was the couple your age?" I asked. "No, they were fifteen years older, I'd say, maybe more." "Did they have any children?" "They had a son, but he died. I didn't see a single picture of him anywhere in the house. You may be asking yourself why I've told you all this." He sat back then and slumped and seemed to be tired suddenly. I had never seen him this way, had never seen him let his posture collapse. It was a different face I was seeing, the inside of his face appearing on the outside, but the voice he spoke with was much the same. "I've said some things tonight that I have never told you before." It was true, he had. "And I have never told them to anyone. You have known me and my parents and have been in the house where I grew up and played in my yard and have seen and heard me all my life and still you are able to listen to me, without understanding why." He had never spoken to me this way before, directly to me, but there was still the web in his words. "You have corrected me when you thought I was not speaking the truth, but you have never come out and called me a liar, even when you thought I was lying. But I was not lying. If my voice could unravel what would be at the middle of it? Not just a word or a few words, but a long string of words would be needed to say what was there. And I want to say those words, I am trying to say some of them. I am an open mouth, a hole screaming in a normal voice. I am the talker and the listener, the guest and the host. I am the son and the dog, the father and mother, the missing and the present, the voice that is flesh and not flesh." He leaned toward me, his voice loud and coming from all over him, and my mouth opened and moved as if about to say his words. "And the sounds I am making must be in you, screaming back at me but unspoken. You can hear them in both of us and it is in these sounds that you will find your need to hear and understand the words I say, your need to find yourself in my words and to understand how you got there. In hearing me you hear yourself, and in some way you know that all that I have said is in some way true, though you cannot believe it could be."

Gone

What happens when you lose your breath? You lose your voice. But your voice goes on inside, the fight goes on inside.

I start talking, but the wind goes out of me, the coughing starts and I can't talk. I can't straighten things out this way. I can't explain anything to anybody. I feel as if I'm drowning.

I'm cold. I've told my daughters this and they say they've turned up the heat, but I can't tell if they have or not. They say they're hot and I say I'm cold. They want the curtains open to get some light in. I don't know what they want light for. I don't want people looking in here. I don't need to see anything, and I've got a lamp if I do. They say light would make me feel better, but having light won't make it easier for me to breathe. I can't stand it here anymore, and I've told them that. They can't take care of me and stay here with me every night. They're tired of me and I don't blame them. They've got lives to lead. Lou's out looking for a place, but it takes time.

Here comes Tara with hot soup on a tray. She thinks I need to eat, but I'm not hungry. Swallowing makes me cough, nothing wants to go down. I've told them all this but you'd think I wasn't talking. All I hear about is food. What I need is sleep, not food. I can't sleep and the doctors won't do anything about it. They give me pills to take, but I stay awake even when I take them. If I get three hours I'm lucky. I'm up all night staring at the walls, not knowing what to do. Anyway, Tara stands over me as I try to eat the soup. It has some vegetables in it that she thinks are good for me. How much good are carrots, squash, and celery going to do me at this point? I choke on a bite and cough until my throat clears. I tell her I don't want any more and I'm not hungry, but she won't listen to me. I eat a few more bites just to keep her off my back and to get her to take away the tray.

When she's satisfied and picks up the tray she asks if she can get me anything. I tell her to bring me a toothpick. I've got a string of celery stuck in my teeth and I don't want to try to wrestle it out with my fingers. I'm out of breath, my lungs are like leather and if I chase this strand of celery around with my tongue or try to suck it out I'll probably exhaust myself. That's what I've come to. Outmuscled by a strand of celery. I hear Tara in the other part of the condo asking Cam where the toothpicks are. Cam is watching a game show and doesn't want to get up and look. I consider shouting to forget the toothpick, but I want the damn thing and I keep quiet.

Tara shows up with a toothpick, and I put it in my mouth and roll my tongue over it, but I can tell right away it isn't right. I don't want a round toothpick, I tell her, handing it back, I want a flat toothpick. The round toothpicks don't fit between my teeth. I tell her the flat ones are in a box in the spice cabinet. Bottom shelf on the left. She rolls her eyes when I'm talking to her, there's enough light in the room to see her face.

She brings the flat toothpick right back in and I thank her and she leaves. I work the celery out and put the toothpick aside to use again. I close my eyes and try to clear my head and let myself drift off. I hear cars going by outside and wonder where they're all going. My driving days are over, my world is shrinking. That person who was out there is receding. The one who went for groceries, the one who shopped the sales and walked the malls doesn't exist anymore. The outside person has fallen away, and what's left? A cougher? A gasper? A voice struggling against a loss of breath?

Often when I close my eyes I see a man walking away from me, bundled in a black overcoat that hangs down to a stone path. Though he keeps walking, he never seems to grow more distant. The path is not flat and he walks slowly to be sure of his footing. He never turns to look at me and I always see him from behind. Where is he headed? What does he sense lies ahead? If he walks for years more, will he reach it?

I must have fallen asleep for a moment, and I wake up when I hear the front door open and Lou talking to his sisters. I hear his footsteps. He comes in the room and tells me he's found a place that looks good to him. He'll give Tara and Cam the address and they can go look at it tomorrow. If they like it, he'll clear it with my HMO. I ask how long that will take. Lou says doctors have to be contacted and medical records have to be faxed. Forms have to filled out and approved at the nursing home. I can't keep track of everything he's saying, but I tell him to get it done as fast he can. He has the rest of the week off, he says, and he'll work on it tomorrow and try to get me in before the weekend. I tell him to go get the records himself and drive them over to whoever wants them. Don't wait for them to look in the fax machine. Put the records in their hands and sit there till they read them. He doesn't want to tell me no and he won't say he'll do it, but I want an answer out of him. Don't wait, I say again. He tells me he'll call around tomorrow and see if people are moving. That's all I'm getting out of him so I drop it.

I tell him I'm cold, and Tara and Cam don't want to keep turning up the heat. Cam says she's already sweating. I can't eat anything, I say, can't sleep, can't get out of bed without running out of breath. Last night I saw shapes on the walls in the middle of the night. The shapes were fuzzy and bright, like luminous insects. I knew they weren't there, but they scared me and I called out for Cam. She didn't hear me so I pulled myself out of bed and tried to make it down the hallway. But I couldn't make it. I fell on the floor, coughing and groaning. Finally Cam came for me, but she couldn't lift me and she didn't know what the problem was. I have to get out of here, I tell Lou. Get me out of here once and for all. I'm never coming back, in case they ask you at this nursing facility. I can't take care of myself and I don't know what to do. No one can make me sleep, and I can't breathe. I'm drowning.

All this talk is wearing me out and I start coughing. I can't hear what Lou is saying but know the gist of it is that he'll do the best he can. I wheeze and try to catch a deep breath. My lungs are just shot, I tell Lou. And this last doctor I went to about my lungs, I go on, never did anything to help me and didn't know enough to help me. He's the one who said I didn't need an oxygen tank to take with me. I said, can't you see I'm out of breath if I take a step? The man is an idiot and I told him so. I didn't want to be insulting, but he made me do it. I told him he didn't know anything about lungs. Lou says he called the doctor's office on the way over in his car, and the nurse told him the doctor would have to see me again before he could give a report to my HMO. I'm not going in there, I say to Lou, I can't. Do they think I can just walk in that building and hop on the elevator? Lou says he told them that and they went back and forth and finally agreed to talk to the doctor about it.

I tell Lou I can't talk any more. I close my eyes and cough, and it hurts my chest. The heart doctor told me after my angioplasty that my chest would keep hurting, don't worry about it, if it gets bad take two nitro tablets. I went back into the hospital a couple of months ago with chest pains. Your lungs are worse than your heart, he told me then, and they'll probably get you before your heart does.

Lou says he's going home to Liv, his wife, who's expecting him for dinner. We hug and he says he hopes I can sleep. I cough as he pulls away, and before he leaves I hear him talking to Cam and Tara about the nursing facility.

I feel like a stick. One hundred and five pounds the last time I weighed. My closet is stuffed with clothes I'll never wear again, and my filing cabinet and desk are stuffed with papers that will be shredded and thrown away. The place will be emptied and sold and the cars outside will keep passing by.

Lou finally got me cleared to go in, and without dragging me into that doctor's office. He stayed on the phone with doctors, the HMO, and the nursing facility until the way was cleared. Hell if I know what all the talk was about. If it had been up to them they never would have let me in, and I'd be lying here dead while they filled out forms and shot faxes back and forth. That's what they like to do. They like to shoot faxes around and push dozens of forms at people to sign and leave messages for people who never answer their phones. If Lou hadn't signed all those forms, I wouldn't have gotten in because I would have been too tired to sign them all. I don't know how these people stay in business. With them it's a way of life to make it difficult for their customers to get through the door.

Lou is here now waiting for the call to give me final approval. I don't know what kind of approval I have now. My bag is packed and in his trunk. Over twenty years in this condo and I'm sick of it. I'm sick of this bed, the smell of the place, the drip in the bathtub, the unfinished paperwork on my desk. Then there's the fat woman upstairs. She spends all day running water. She takes four or five baths a day. When she shifts, I can hear the tub squeaking. She washes clothes constantly. I don't know how many dirty clothes she can have or if she just washes the same ones over and over. The load in her washer keeps shifting and I hear the machine dancing all over the floor. During the summer the air conditioner runs all day long. She probably takes all those baths to warm herself up. When her husband comes home from work they start screwing. I hear the bed going kathump, kathump, kathump. I don't know what he's doing to her up there but it takes them a long time to get to the end of whatever it is. And when they do get to the end, I hear it.

The phone rings and Lou picks it up. It's the call we've been waiting for. He nods, says yes a few times and then hangs up and says we're ready to go. My cane is by the bed. I tell him I don't know if I can get out to the car, he might have to carry me. He tells me I can do it, but how does he know what I can do? He just doesn't want to put me over his shoulder and carry me out, and I can't blame him for that. Tara's at work so she can't help and we don't know what happened to Cam. She was here when Lou arrived. He and I were in the bedroom talking and he went out to get me some water and found that Cam was gone. She hadn't even turned off the TV. Lou walked all over the grounds looking for her, looking for her car in the parking areas. No Cam. He came back empty-handed and asked me if Cam had gotten mad about something. I told him that some kind of anger was always jerking Cam around.

I sit up on the edge of the bed and Lou hands me my cane. I tell him to let me sit till I stop puffing. I catch my breath, then push myself up and begin moving down the hallway. I'm shaky as I round the corner into the living room, and I head for the couch. I sit and tell Lou I'm taking a pause before I go the rest of the way. Lou sits next to me. I'm heaving with the effort to breathe. I can see through the glass door that his car is parked straight ahead at the end of the walkway. I ask him if the car door is unlocked. I don't want to stand there leaning on his car while he gets his key out and so forth. He says it's unlocked, and I say I'm ready to go. I get up with my weight on the cane and Lou hurries ahead to open the door. I watch my step and go out into the light. I hear him locking up behind me. I can't think how many days it has been since I've been out. I watch the steps and keep moving, my eyes on Lou's car. He takes my arm and helps me, and when we near his car he moves ahead of me. He opens the door and helps me in and pulls the seat belt across my body and fastens it. The cane is across my lap and I struggle to breathe. He shuts the door and goes around, gets in and starts the car. We're off.

It takes me a minute or two to realize that I forgot my glasses. He asks if I want him to go back for them and I tell him no, I don't need to read anything anyway. He can get them later and bring them to me. My chest hurts and I can't stop groaning. He asks if I'm all right. I tell him I just need to catch my breath, but it's hard for me to catch it. I hope I don't make a fool of myself when I go in this place, I tell Lou. He says I won't, and he'll go in and get somebody to bring out a wheelchair for me. I won't have to walk.

They're waiting for me, he says. I hope they don't laugh at me, I say. He says there's no reason for them to laugh.

It's a short way, ten minutes to the facility. Lou parks and runs in for this person who's supposed to help. I can see them in the mirror when they come out. He's with a big fat woman pushing a wheelchair. I hope she doesn't fall on me. I'd be crushed.

Lou swings the door open and she reaches in and helps me into the chair. She rolls me forward, and Lou gets my bag from his trunk and catches up with us. She pushes me up a ramp and through the front door. Some of the residents look dazed, but most of them seem only vaguely aware that I'm there. A couple of them nod at me. We go down hallways, passing from carpet to linoleum and through a dining room where a number of residents are slowly eating, some of them talking. Ahead, a fat woman crosses our path. There's a skinny one, I say to Lou. He's worried she might have heard me and I say I don't think she could hear it, but if she did, so what? She knows she's fat and it's not my fault she is. I'm not the one who fills her plate and eats it.

The woman pushing the chair tells us we're almost there. A man at the nurses' station waves at me and I wave back. She pushes the chair ahead until she turns into a room on the left, my name on the plate outside the door, first name and last name both misspelled. I point it out on the way in and Lou says he'll get it fixed. The woman gets my shoes off and gets me in the bed. I tell her I appreciate it, and she leaves us. I pant and cough, my chest heaving. I'm shaking. I reach for Lou and pull him to my chest. I'm so tired of this fucking shit, I say to him.

I was cold in the room, and the vent in the ceiling kept blowing on me. They said they couldn't change the temperature in my room without changing it in the whole wing. No one else had a problem with it, according to them, so there was nothing they could do. I kept complaining, though, and one of the aides moved my bed and got a square of cardboard and some duct tape and covered the vent. He was the only one who'd listen to me.

I don't know what's going on with my pills. Some of them I'm used to, the blood thinner and whatnot, but a doctor came around to see me the first day and she prescribed a couple of new ones. I don't know what they are, and the people who give them to me don't seem to know either. I ask them how they can give somebody a pill without knowing what it is. It doesn't make sense. If I refuse to take the pills, they stand there and argue with me until I swallow them. Lou called the doctor for an explanation of the new pills, but I still don't know if they're giving me what they're supposed to give me. They give me a sleeping pill, but I still wake up in the night. I tell them I need another one and they say they can't let me have it without word from the doctor. Lou told the doctor I want a second sleeping pill, but she doesn't want to do it that way. She doubled the dose of the first sleeping pill, but I still wake up.

I don't know how to get through to these people. They make faces and talk back to me when I complain. They don't like me because I speak my mind. There's a fat man who comes in here with pills sometimes and I can't understand a word he says. I told him I've got no problem with wherever he comes from but I have to be able to understand him. He understands what I'm saying and he talks louder. I don't hear well, but it doesn't help anything for him to say whatever it is he's saying in a louder voice. Cam was here the other day when he came in and she could understand him, but she can't stay here all day waiting to act as an interpreter. I hesitate to take pills from this guy because I have no idea what he's telling me about them. He had one that looked new to me and I didn't have the slightest idea what he was telling me about it. How do I know I'm not taking a pill that's meant for another person? Then he asked me something. Do you want to order, I thought he asked me. He said it again. I wondered if he thought we were sitting in a restaurant someplace. Someone else came in and he repeated it. He was asking me if I wanted water.

These pathologists and therapists who come by are another thing. They drive me crazy asking all these questions, and I get tired and winded answering them all. The speech pathologist won't get off the idea of putting thickener in all my fluids and she won't listen to me when I say I don't want the thickener. She tells me the thickener makes it easier for me to swallow. I don't think it does and I told her that, but she thinks she knows better. I asked if it was her or me who was swallowing this stuff. She didn't care what I said. She put me down for thickener. She wants all my food cut up in little bites so I won't choke on it. I told her I'd go one better. I wouldn't eat the food at all because I couldn't taste it anyway. When I could taste it, I wished I couldn't. Whenever she comes in here she gets me agitated. She's always telling me what to do.

Lou called and talked to her and he thinks it all sounds reasonable. He says I have to eat and I have a hard time disagreeing with that until I see a plate of the food they put in front of me. I tell him that sometimes I can't tell what I've got on my plate. Is it grits, potatoes, applesauce, or pudding? Even when I taste it, I still can't tell half the time. Lou was here the other day when they served me a meal. I wouldn't touch it, but he picked up the fork and ate half of it himself. He said it wasn't great but it wasn't bad. He thought he'd get me to eat the rest of it, but I wasn't going to let him work me into a corner with that one.

Lou and Tara have both talked to the nurses about my pills. They seem to think the nurses are doing the best they can. I heard Lou talking to one of them in the hall. He seemed to be apologizing for me. He said I was frustrated and he hoped I wasn't being rude to them. I shouted that I wasn't being rude to anybody but I wanted to know what pills I was taking. I shouted that I wanted to be able to look at a plate of food and tell the difference between grits and mashed potatoes.

I can't stop thinking about this place and all the problems. I complained to Cam about it and she got mad. You don't want to get Cam mad at you. I don't want her going to the nurses' station and throwing a fit, or worse. She might get me thrown out of here. She wants me out, but I've told her I'm not leaving. She's mad at Lou and Tara for putting me in here. I told her not to blame them. Cam could have looked at the place too, but she decided not to come by. The way she has it, Lou took charge and didn't care what she thought. I told her I had to get out of that condo, but she doesn't want to hear it.

I choke on a bite and have a coughing fit. Cam is here, and she goes into a spin and runs down the hall to get some help. A nurse runs in and she slaps my back as I cough. She calms me down and stays with me until I stop coughing. She gives me some thickened water to drink. I tuck my chin, the way the speech pathologist taught me, and swallow. I get settled, but I'm weak and out of breath. I push the tray back and Cam says I need to get out of here. I tell her I won't be better if I go somewhere else. This is the way I am. After I was in the hospital for the angioplasty I went to a care facility to recover. Cam says I got better at that place and I'm not getting better at this one. This situation is different, I try to tell Cam. My lungs are getting worse, I can't swallow sometimes, and there's nothing they can do about it. I'm ready to go anyway, I tell her. I've lived my life. I should be getting better, Cam tells me, and she won't listen to me when I disagree with her.

I'm picking at my lunch when the speech pathologist comes in, and while she's here I choke again. I can't breathe, and I grip her arm and cough worse than last night during the fit I had with Cam. I try to force the food up with the coughs, the pain in my chest worse than when I had my heart attack. I finally bring it up and swallow and lie back, exhausted, holding her arm. She tries to relax me as I struggle to catch my breath.

Lou says they're taking me to the hospital tomorrow for some kind of barium swallow test. I tell him I'm not going. I don't want to go near a hospital, I'll end up worse, there's no better place to get any infection known to man than a hospital. What are they going to do to help me? More of the same shit, I say. Lou again tells me that I need to eat. He tells me I weigh less than a hundred pounds and I say so what, how much does he want me to weigh? And what is the barium swallow test going to tell us that we don't already know? That I can't swallow? I don't need a test. He says they'll take a picture of what's happening when I swallow, but he admits he doesn't know if it will do me any good. I ask him why I should do it then. He says the speech pathologist said that food could be getting in my lungs. That could lead to an infection and I could get pneumonia. I can't see what the test will help, but I can't get him off it, and they've already made an appointment for me at the hospital.

When they come for me it's raining. Two big guys strap me down on a stretcher with wheels and push me out my door and down the hallway. I hear rain on the roof and I ask them if they're going to cover me before we go outside. One of them shrugs and looks at the other one. He breaks off and the one who's left with me stops at the door to the outside and waits for him.

The guy comes back with a clear sheet of plastic and drapes it over me. I look like I'm coming back from the dry cleaners. I tell this genius, who is so big he could pick me up over his head and twirl me around, not to put it over my face because I can't breathe. He pulls the plastic down and tucks it under my chin.

They have a kind of van waiting at the curb. They roll me up the back, pop the legs on the stretcher up, and push me in.

At the hospital I meet a new speech pathologist and I ask her if she's seen or heard from my son. Lou said he would take off work and be here when I had the test, but she says she hasn't seen him. I sit down at the machine that takes pictures of my neck and throat as I swallow. She tells me what she's doing, but she uses too many words I don't know and I can't keep up with what she's saying. She gives me barium to swallow and then some pudding, and I cough and choke on both of them. I keep coughing whatever I swallow back up, trying to get it down. She asks me something, but I can't hear her and can't ask her to repeat it because of the coughing.

She tells me what she thinks I should do, but it's hard for me to follow and I tell her to go look for Lou. He'll understand what she's saying. I hear the words therapy and tube. She asks me a question and waits for an answer, but she's talking too fast for me. I tell her I'm tired and out of breath. Maybe she can talk to Lou later.

She wheels me out to the waiting room in back. I feel myself fading.

Lou wakes me up, his hand on my shoulder. He asks if I just got here. I didn't just get here, I say, I've been here for a long time. Someone is with him, I see, a woman with a clipboard and a form on it. She says she's from admitting. I ask her why she's admitting me when I've already finished my test. I may be confused, I tell her, but I know that you should be admitted before you have your test. Lou says he's been waiting out front for an hour and a half. They have a waiting room for this department and the people at that desk told him I hadn't arrived yet. He went to admitting and they had no record of me. They suggested he take a seat. He called the nursing facility and they said I was on my way. He'd been pacing, wondering what happened to me. Then this woman from admitting called out our last name. She took my information from him and brought him back here, and she's surprised to see me too. Lou wants to know why he wasn't told I was here. He wanted to be with me when I had the test and to hear what the pathologist said about my condition. I tell Lou that all these medical people care about is running tests they charge to the system and asking people a bunch of questions so they can fill in their forms. I tell the clipboard-holding woman from admitting that I'm cold in this room and ask her what she's going to do about it. She says she'll let us talk to a supervisor.

She takes off and soon a guy with one of those pale green V-necked shirts struts up. Lou asks why he waited out front for an hour and a half and no one out there knew enough to tell him I was in back having a test. This guy gives Lou a smug look and says no one there knew I was in the back having the test. Lou says he asked if I was in the back having the test and they didn't check before telling him no. This guy looks put out with Lou. His look says that Lou doesn't understand the way a hospital works. He explains that I was brought through the back way for my convenience rather than through the front way in admitting, which would have taken longer. Lou wants to know why the front didn't know what the back was doing. The guy says because the people in the back were busy taking care of me. Lou then says he wants to talk to the speech pathologist who gave me the test. The supervisor says he'll see if she's available. Lou tells him as he walks off that he'll stay here until she is available.

We wait a minute or so before the speech pathologist appears over my shoulder. Lou walks away with her and says he'll be back after he hears her report.

Lou gets back to my room before I do. He hops up from a chair when he sees me. The guys wheel me in and help me up and into the bed and then they leave. Lou says when he got through talking to the speech pathologist he came back out to the waiting room where I'd been, but I was gone. I tell him that some attendant pushed me into another waiting room. I went to sleep again and when I woke up they were putting me back in the van. I tell Lou I'm tired and cold and I'm not going back to the hospital. He says I'll have to go back. They want to put a feeding tube in my stomach. They call it a peg. Nobody's putting any peg in my stomach, I tell him. He says I have to have a peg to get nutrition and hydration. My epiglottis doesn't work, the speech pathologist told him. I remember her saying something about an epiglottis, but I don't know what an epiglottis is and I couldn't understand her. Lou keeps on about the nutrition and I give up and say I'll go. I don't know if I will, but he won't leave me alone until I say it. I ask him how long the peg will be in and he says they may not be able to take it out. Never? I ask. That's what he thinks they told him. I don't want to talk about it. I ask him to stay with me awhile longer. They bring in my dinner and he helps me eat it. A piece of fish and green beans. I'm starved and I eat the whole thing without coughing. I can't figure this stuff out. When I finish I can't stand the sight of the plate and Lou pulls it away from me.

I drop off to sleep, and when I wake up he's gone.

I have a bad night. I'm constipated, my butt hurts, and the softener they're giving me doesn't help. I call Lou to see if he can get in touch with the doctor. It's a Saturday morning and I figure he's at home. When he hears my voice on the recorder he picks up. I can tell by the way he sounds that he's not happy and I ask him what's wrong. He's had a bad night and so has Tara. When he got home he was telling Liv about our day at the hospital, and while he was talking Cam called. She had some rock music on loud in the background and she made retching sounds into the receiver. Lou keeps his ringer off and waits to hear who's calling before he picks up. In this case, he didn't pick up. After she finished retching, Cam turned the music down and began a tirade against Lou. The worst excuse for a brother, the worst excuse for a son, the F-word over and over, the rage, the promise that he wouldn't be safe for the rest of his life, he would never know when she would come out to his house, and there was nothing he could do to stop her. She'd called him back repeatedly in the middle of the night saying she was on her way over. After the second call he got the police out to his house. She called while the officer was there and he listened to one of her messages. The next call came quickly and the policeman picked up the phone on the first ring, thinking he would talk to Cam. But that call was from Tara and the officer handed the phone to Lou. Tara said that Cam had been calling her with threatening messages. She'd come out to Tara's house, had thrown three dozen eggs at it, then turned her music way up, stripped down to her waist and danced topless on top of her car while shouting obscenities at Tara. Tara also called the police but it took almost thirty minutes for someone to get there. By then, Cam was gone. The officer made a report, but he told Tara he couldn't do anything to Cam. The vandalism was minor, there was no law against someone dancing topless, and he hadn't witnessed anything that had happened. But when the officer was walking back to his cruiser, Cam pulled up and got out of her car. She told him that I was dying and she was the only one in the family who would do anything to help me. Lou and Tara didn't care about me, she said, and they had put me away someplace to watch me die.

The policeman who came to Lou's house wrote up the complaint but said the threats would have to be more direct and severe before any action could be taken against Cam. Lou and Tara both unplugged their phones.

I tell Lou that Cam just wants to show off. She's mad at him and Tara because she doesn't like the care I'm getting and she blames them because they're the ones who looked at the place. She feels she was left out of it and that Lou doesn't care what she thinks. Just ignore her, I tell him, but Lou doesn't want to ignore her. Liv is upset and he's upset. He didn't leave Cam out, he says. She chose not to go in for a look and that's not his fault. I tell him again to forget about it. Cam likes to blow off steam and that's just the way she is. Lou says Tara slept next door at her neighbor's, and I say that Tara doesn't need to sleep at her neighbor's. Cam won't do anything. She just wants to act like a big shot. She's been mad at me and called me up screaming and cursing, but I ignored her. Don't let her know it bothers you, I tell Lou. I also say that I'm constipated and none of these people here care about it. I ask him to call the doctor. He thinks her office is closed for the weekend, he says, but he'll call the nurses' station and see if he can get them to help me. I hang up. I've heard enough of it. I think of calling Cam, but she never answers the phone and I don't want to tell it to her recorder. Nobody can straighten Cam out anyway. She does whatever she wants to and nobody can tell her anything.

———

I can't sleep worrying about it. Cam didn't come in to see me and she comes almost every day. I wonder if she's out there terrorizing somebody.

Lou calls early. Cam left a message on his answering machine yesterday afternoon. She said she'd changed the locks on my condo so that he and Tara won't be able to get in. She later left another message that said her lawyer will be contacting the Medicaid lawyer Lou has been working with for me. She threatened to have her lawyer examine any transactions that Lou authorizes or makes himself. She told him she'd see him in court. Lou and I both know that Cam has a lawyer. I don't know all the trouble she gets into, but she's had a monitoring device attached to her ankle a couple of times and once she spent a month in jail because of a dispute with a neighbor. I don't ask her about her legal troubles. I don't want to know the details.

Lou adds that the police have been out to his house again. In another call, this one at three in the morning, Cam said during a barrage of profanity that he was killing me and she was going to kill him. She also called Tara and said she had a 9mm that she was going to use on Lou. The officer at Lou's house made a report of the threat and is going to turn it over to a detective. Lou says he's unplugging his phone when he and Liv go to bed and wants me to know that if I call while they're asleep I won't be able to reach him. I ask him what I should do if I need him. He says he won't know I'm calling until he plugs in his phone in the morning. He then says that Cam is angry because of all the complaining I've done about the food and care at the facility. He wants me to call and tell her to leave him and Tara alone. I answer that I don't want to do that. I don't want Cam mad at me. She's threatened me a dozen times, I tell him, and it doesn't mean a thing. She's said more than once she was going to kill me and I'm still here. Cam just likes to scare people, I say. He wants to know why I don't want her mad at me, then. He says I should call her and tell her that if she doesn't like where I'm staying she should look for a better place, then sign all the papers to get me into it and drive me there herself. I tell him I'm not going anywhere and that Cam doesn't know how to look for a place. Lou says if I don't call her, he won't work with the Medicaid lawyer and he won't be the executor of my estate. Who'll do it then? I ask. Get Cam to help you, he answers. He asks why he and Tara should suffer for what they've done to try to help me? All I do is complain about it, he says. Don't do this, I say. You're the oldest and you should be in charge of these things. She's threatening to kill me, he says, and you're not doing anything about it. I can't do anything about it, I tell him. You're throwing me in the trash. If you do this I won't eat or drink again. I'll starve myself. That's up to you, he says, and hangs up.

My hands shake as I call Cam. I know she won't answer, but her recorder comes on. Please come to the phone, Cam. Please come to the phone. I have something I need to say to you. Please call or come in to see me. I need to talk to you.

I turn off the phone and put it in my lap. I start a coughing fit and struggle to breathe. I want some water but I don't want to choke on it. I grab the water bottle and tuck my chin. I sip and breathe, sip and breathe. It goes down. I put the bottle down and lean back and close my eyes.

Cam comes in that night, a knotted look on her face. She's angry but she's also worried. She says I sounded bad on the phone. I tell her Lou has told me what she's doing to him and Tara. They both called the cops on me, she says, spitting it out. What do you expect them to do? I ask. She wants to know what I expect her to do. She says they deserve it for what they've done to me. They haven't done anything to me, I say, and you can't treat people that way. You can't threaten your brother and sister. I'm telling you to leave them alone.

I'm out of breath and it makes her mad to see how weak I am. She blames it on Lou and Tara. She complains that they've upset me. They're not upsetting me, I tell her, you're upsetting me. Decent people don't do what you're doing. If you don't stop it I won't have anything more to do with you. I won't put up with it, Cam, this is no time for it. Cam shouts that she's never going to leave them alone. She's outraged they don't keep their phones unplugged and then get mad when she calls them. In her mind, this makes them hypocrites. She says I'm afraid of Lou and Tara, and I tell her I'm not afraid of them, I'm afraid of her. They've turned you against me, she says. She yanks up her purse and leaves. Don't do it again, I rise up and shout.

I put my face in my hands and rub it. My chest rattles and feels as if someone is sitting on it. I'm drowning. I don't know what to do with Cam. I never have.

I take in a few breaths and call Lou. I talked to Cam, I say. I did the best I could. I told her that if she doesn't stop calling you and Tara I'm through with her. She knew I meant it and she stomped out. I don't know what she'll do now. I can't control Cam.

I feel desperate talking to Lou, wondering what he'll say. He believes I did the best I could, he says. He didn't think Cam should get by with what she did without a word from me. I'm the closest one to her and if she'd listen to anyone it would be me. He says he'll keep working with the Medicaid lawyer and he'll handle my estate and look for a different place for me if I want him to. I tell him I don't have the strength to move and even if the food is better at another place it isn't going to do me any good. Neither is anything else. He thanks me for talking to Cam. He knows it was hard for me. He tells me he loves me and I tell him the same. I say that if Cam comes out there, get her thrown in jail if he can. That's where she belongs and don't worry if it's going to bother me. My words are slurring. My mouth is dry and my chest hurts. I tell him I can't talk any more today. He tells me to get some rest.

———————

I try to sleep, but it's too hard to breathe. My lungs feel as if they're made of lead. I stretch my neck, trying to get some air. I know it's there but I can't breathe it in. My heart is bothering me. I don't know what to do. If I call for help they'll drag me off to the hospital and start asking me questions about how I feel and giving me one test after another. But my breathing keeps getting worse, and I get scared and call for someone.

He gets to me quick. It's early in the morning, still dark out. He can see how hard it is for me to breathe. He tells me to hang on and he'll call for an ambulance to come for me. He leaves. I almost ask him to stay, but what can he do if he does?

He comes back before long and says the ambulance is on the way. Don't wake everybody up, I say, and he says not to worry about that. I ask him to let Lou and Tara know.

———————

Things begin to happen fast. They lug me out to the ambulance and get me to the hospital and put me in a waiting room. Tara gets there a few minutes after I do. She says she's tried to call Lou but his phone just rings. I tell her he's got it unplugged because of Cam. She asks if she should drive over to his house to get him. Round-trip, it would be well over an hour. I tell her he'll plug in his phone when he gets up.

———————

In ICU they put an oxygen mask over my mouth and nose. I don't know what all I'm hooked up to, and when they try to explain it to me I tell them I appreciate what they're doing but I can't understand most of it and what I do understand I can't remember for even a minute. They talk to Tara.

Lou is already here. I see him outside the room talking to the lung specialist they assigned to me. I hear the doctor tell him that my x-rays look bad, the last stages of pulmonary fibrosis. He told me the same thing, and I said I knew it without the x-ray.

Lou comes in and asks if he should call Cam. I say that unless Cam has apologized to him and Tara, I don't want her coming around here. She can't treat people like trash and get away with it. He tells me he's going to contact security and let them know about her. If she calls the nursing facility they might tell her where I am and it could set her off.

A security guard with a thick chest and a small spiral notepad shows up and Lou tells him a brief version of Cam's adventures. The guard asks Lou for a description of Cam. Short, Lou says, brown hair, large breast implants. She owns a gun and drives a red BMW. The guard repeats the description and raises his eyebrows when he mentions the implants.

After he leaves, Lou and Tara talk to me, but it's a struggle to try to answer them. My words are hard to make out and I have to repeat myself. The lung doctor comes in and says something I can't hear to Lou. Lou comes to the bed and leans over me. He asks if I want to be resuscitated. I tell him no. I just want to make sure you understand, Lou says. If you stop breathing, they won't try to bring you back. Is that what you want? I don't want anything, I tell him. Just let me go.

The doctor steps toward me and says he'll continue giving me antibiotics, but he'll tell the nurses to mark me DNR. He grips my arm and then walks out.

A minute later a nurse comes in with a DNR label to strap around my wrist. She doesn't seem to like putting it on me, and as she leaves she tells me I can change my mind if I want to. I push myself up and lift up the plastic mask. I'm not changing my mind, I say as strong as I can. No way.

I go in and out. I can't talk and get exhausted if I try. I imagine Cam showing up and waving a gun around at everybody. I see things moving in the walls.

I breathe into the mask and close my eyes. I don't have the strength to think or be angry anymore.

I know they're there. I hear them but don't know what they're saying. It's enough to hear their voices and feel their hands. I'm slipping into space but the space is nowhere.

I see the man in the black overcoat stumble on the path. I near him and feel myself slipping into him as his breathing winds down and stops. I rise as if floating and start again. There is no path, only open space. I drift ahead. My fear releases me.

For the last time, I don't know what to do. I don't care.

Invite

For over forty years I'd remembered a question I'd been asked at a party I went to in the eighth grade. I was happy and surprised that I'd been asked to come. The girl hosting the party was popular and friendly to me but I didn't think of myself as being in her statusphere, which is what I called it in those days. I arrived and was saying hello all around and one of the guys there, a guy I was in a couple of classes with, gave me a questioning look and said, "What are you doing here?" The emphasis on the word "you" hurt, especially since other people heard the question. "I was invited," I answered, but the questioner chuckled in my face, disbelieving, and kept looking at me as if I didn't belong there.

Over the years, sometimes during the night when I lay awake, the memory would return and trouble me. Sometimes when I was sitting in my office at work, if I had an idle moment or was having a bad day, the question would come to mind and wait to be answered. I'd told my wife about it a time or two when we were sharing painful memories, but no one else had ever heard the story.

I hadn't seen the guy since high school and had no idea what had become of him, but one night my wife and I were at a crowded book signing party at the home of some people we'd never met and I saw a man across the room, in a jumble of other faces, who looked to me to be the guy. He looked prosperous and seemed to be enjoying a laugh with the group he was talking with. The sight of him angered me, and the anger hit me like a blow. I could no longer hear the man beside me, who'd been talking to me about antiques. I had a glass of wine in my hand and I tried to take a drink, but after I got the wine in my mouth I couldn't swallow on the first try and didn't know if I'd be able to get it down my throat. I feared I'd have to spit it back in the glass. Worse, in my mind, was that when my wife saw me she'd know that something was bothering me, she could always tell, and she'd ask me what had happened and I'd have a hard time not telling her. I always told her, but in this case I didn't want to come out with it at the party. For one thing she might want to make sure he was the same person who'd asked the question and for another she might get angry and say something to him. We didn't know many people at the party but we did have two friends there, a couple, whose daughter had written the book that was being celebrated. My wife might think it was a good idea to ask them if they knew the man's name and who he was, and if they didn't know they might try to find out, which could lead back to me and end up with the guy approaching me and extending his hand and saying my name. I thought of walking out, but I couldn't leave the party and come back an hour and a half later. My wife would worry about me, there'd be an uproar, and an explanation to our friends would be required. I wouldn't want to give them the real explanation and I didn't want to lie to them.

Meanwhile, the man next to me was still talking about antiques. I didn't see how I could just turn and walk away from him, but that left me in the line of sight of the questioner. I began to think that all my life I'd been sensitive to being questioned and had always dreaded questions I didn't have an answer for. Questions I couldn't answer seemed to go right through my spine and into my bloodstream. Was my dread a hangover from the question the man across the room had asked me? Why shouldn't I go up to him and ask him what he was doing there? Where did he get the nerve to ask me what I was doing at that party? I told myself that I shouldn't get near him, because there was no telling what I'd do or say.

Then I saw my wife coming toward me with a worried look. She'd seen my face and that was enough. She took my arm and joined me in listening to the antiques enthusiast and smiled at him, trying to convey a desire to say something to me. He got the drift and closed his story and left us alone, and after he was gone, my wife immediately asked me what was wrong. I was reluctant to tell her, reluctant to open up a painful subject, and I didn't know if I could get into it without attracting attention to us. My face might look too twisted for a book signing party. I asked her to step outside so that I could explain.

We passed the book signing table on our way to the front door, our friends' daughter smiling and talking to people, her supply of books almost down to nothing. When we were outside I told her that the questioner was at the party and she wanted to know if I was sure it was him, people changed in that many years and it could just be someone who resembled him. I nodded and said that it was him, something about his ears and the way he was looking at people with his nose up in the air made me sure it was the same guy. She offered to find out more, to confirm his identity, and I said I didn't want her poking around and that I thought I should leave the party. I couldn't face the guy, I said, I knew it was out of all proportion, but it sickened me to think of being in the same house with that man. I suggested she tell our friends that I was taken ill and that I'd either come back for her or they could bring her home. I told her that if he recognized me he might try to talk to me. I didn't want to talk to him, to hear about his successes or his kids' successes, if he had any kids, and my greatest fear was that he'd ask me the same question all over again and I might hurt him. My wife said that I wasn't going to hurt him, I'd never hurt anybody, not like that, and I wasn't going to start beating people up at my age. I answered that I didn't want to upset myself further by thinking about hurting him. I wanted to be out of that house and felt better already being out in the open air. She then said that we had to go back in and she would stand beside me the whole time we were there, until we left in the normal course of events or until he left. I shouldn't be running from this guy, she told me, I had nothing to be ashamed of, he was the one who had something to be ashamed of asking me that. I could see that she was angry at the thought of this guy being in the house and I asked her to promise me that she wouldn't say anything to him about what he'd asked me and that she wouldn't ask around about him. She promised and we started back in.

When we were inside the door she wanted me to point the guy out to her, but I didn't want to go looking for him and didn't want him to observe me pointing him out. I also said I didn't want to see him or to let him see me. I told my wife that I'd rather lock myself in the bathroom than let this guy take a look at me, even if he'd have no idea who he was looking at. My wife told me that I should step back and put this in perspective.

"Now where is the son of a bitch," she said then, so we went looking for him, creeping around like some furtive detectives.

Finally I saw him as we came around a corner into the den. He was in the kitchen, wine in one hand, leaning on a countertop with the other. He was nodding as if he knew well that what he was listening to was the total truth, and his head turned as he sensed movement to his left. It was our movement he sensed, and I turned my face away from him in as natural a way as I could manage. My wife immediately asked if that was him. I told her not to look back quick, but he was the guy leaning on the counter in the kitchen. She cut her eyes toward him and said he was looking at us, but he'd turned his head away and seemed to show no sign of recognition.

As I was suggesting that we stroll out of the room our friends spotted us and one of them said my name. They began talking to us about getting together for dinner after the party and I tried to get a smile going and shifted my back toward the kitchen. My wife said we'd be happy to go to dinner after the party and the discussion turned to restaurant options. At that moment I couldn't imagine swallowing anything, but I nodded at whatever choices they mentioned and considered making a detour to the bathroom. It unnerved me to be standing so close to the guy and I could hear his voice behind me going on about politics. From what he said I could tell he was on the wrong side of the issue, and in my mind I began to argue with him about it. I felt an urge to shout out my answer to him, but I knew that to do so would have a dreadful effect.

Our friends were looking at me, I became aware, sensing that I was troubled. They wanted to know if I was all right, if I was feeling ill. My wife answered for me because I was stuck for a reply, and the question seemed to threaten me. I knew they weren't out to browbeat me, but the thought that they wanted an answer hit my nervous system. I started to squirm and felt three different places on my face that needed scratching. I started to lift the hand holding the wine glass and almost threw wine in my face. I couldn't seem to lift my left arm well enough to feel confident that I could zero in on the places that were itching so I just let them itch away at me. My armpits were wet and I feared that sweat would soon begin to trickle down from my hairline, onto my forehead and down the back of my neck. The appearance of that much sweat would provoke more questions and I wouldn't want to answer them. I imagined the guy strolling up with a big smile, nose in the air, and asking me what I was doing at the party. "I was invited," I told him, and I imagined my wife leaning against me to prop me up. I could still think of no answer to give our friends, something to add to what my wife had said, except to assure them that I was fine, which I knew they would not believe. I looked at them, on the verge of serving up some lie, when I saw in their faces that someone they didn't know was approaching me from behind and it came to me what must be about to happen. I heard the questioner say my name, and then he was stepping around my left shoulder and leaning in for a close look at my face. He extended his hand and my wife grabbed my right arm to steady me. The wine sloshed in the glass but the tide did not rise over the edge. I put the wine glass in my other hand and then gripped his right hand fiercely, remembering that he was one of those who sought to pulverize the hand he was shaking. I nodded that I was the person he thought I was.

Then he said, "What—"

"We're friends of the —" my wife interrupted, saying the names of our friends and pointing to them.

"The parents of the author then," he said, as if my wife had correctly anticipated his question.

He didn't bother to explain his connection with anyone at the party, but he looked at me and asked how long it had been since we'd seen each other. I shrugged and did not make eye contact.

"So what do you do to occupy yourself?" he asked.

I didn't want him evaluating what I did for a living or to offer him any encouragement to ask me more questions. I looked up and stared at him and didn't answer, suppressing images of wiping the smile off his face. His face took on a different aspect and he stared back at me. Our friends stared at me and I didn't know if my wife was staring at me or at him or anybody. A woman who I assumed was his wife came up then and looked at both of our faces. She must have seen the staring match from wherever she'd been and wanted to know what was going on. She said his name and I bristled at the sound of it. He gave me a chuckle, the same chuckle he'd given me at the party years ago, and then withdrew with his wife.

I didn't like his chuckle, didn't like the word chuckle. The word chuckle annoyed me and I didn't want this guy I hadn't seen in over forty years leaving me with his chuckle.

"Not a former friend of yours, I take it," our friend, the husband, said.

"A bad memory," I answered.

I excused myself and went to the table where the wine was being served. The bartender refilled my glass, and as he did so I shook my right arm to help the blood circulate. My wife had been gripping it and it had gone numb. The bartender gave my glass back to me and I stood there with it a little too long before moving aside to let the next person in line be served.

I walked to the living room and took a seat. Not many people were in the living room, and I hoped that I could sit without speaking to anyone or answering any questions and let my armpits dry and my mind return to its usual temperature. I'd been sitting there for less than a minute when the questioner's wife, armed with a freshly filled wine glass, came into the room as if she'd been looking for me and sat in the chair next to mine.

"I don't know what my husband did to you," she began, leaning toward me with an air of confidentiality, a trace of a slur in her voice. "But it probably wasn't anything he hasn't done to a lot of other people, including his first two wives. I appreciate the way you stood up to him, and I just wanted to let you know that I am available to talk."

At that point she put a business card on the small table between us, and I saw that she'd written some information on the back of it. She then began to rub her leg and her hand moved slowly up to her knee. She was still leaning toward me when the questioner appeared through the same doorway she'd entered from. His eyes went to the business card and he charged straight up to us and snatched the card off the table and read it. He glanced at me and put the card in his pocket.

"I don't know what your beef is with me," he said, "but whatever it is, I don't see why it would lead you to make contact with my wife."

"I haven't said a word to her since she walked in the room," I told him. "I have never said anything to her in my life and don't care to." I was almost out of breath by the time I finished.

"What are you doing here?" he asked her.

"Oh, your favorite question. I came in here to talk with the man who ignored you in front of those people. Obviously he knows you well."

"I haven't seen him since high school," he said.

My wife came into the room then, but from the other side, and I could tell by the way she approached us that she'd been wondering where I was.

"His wife tried to talk to me," I told her, "and they're having an argument about it."

Several people nearby were beginning to take notice that something might be afoot.

"So what is it then?" the questioner asked. "What's this about? Let's clear it up."

The room seemed to be closing in on me, and the wine was turning against my stomach. I set the glass down on the table, then stood and took my wife's arm, and we left the living room. We talked about what to do next and decided to go out to the covered back porch, where we found some empty seats together.

"I hate all this," I said after a moment. "If he comes out here we'll have to leave. I can't have him chasing me around the house."

She looked back inside.

"Is he coming?"

"I don't see him. But I don't think he'll come after you. He understands you don't want to talk to him. I wouldn't be surprised if they've already left."

But no, there he came. My wife saw him first and got up and went toward him, cutting him off at the doorway as two couples made their way out past them. I looked around and saw only three other people on the porch, and they were involved in their own conversation.

"I just want to ask him something," I heard the questioner say. "Does he want me to beg him?"

How was my wife supposed to answer that?

"Let him out here," I said. "I'm sick of it. I'm tired of avoiding him."

She let him pass and he stood in front of me. I still didn't want him anywhere near me, but the best way to get rid of him seemed to be to give him an answer. I kept it as brief as I could, maybe two or three sentences.

"No matter how I explain it you'll have questions," I said at the end, "but I don't want to answer your questions."

"That's it?"

"That's a question," I said, and I didn't like it that he'd asked. I wanted to ask him what he was implying, but I didn't want to tell him not to ask me questions and then turn around and ask him one, and I didn't want to hear his answer or to hear that he thought the story was pathetic.

"I don't remember saying it, but I believe you. It was rude. I'm sorry," he said. "Can I go home now?"

Again I didn't like the question, didn't know what to answer and didn't know what he meant by it. Why was he asking me if he could go home when he knew that I would have preferred he not come out there in the first place?

"Please don't ask me questions," I repeated.

"You want me to leave you alone, don't you? You thought I was looking down at you. I probably was. You go through a few marriages, you try to learn some things."

I saw him more clearly then, saw that he was slightly pudgy and had a comb-over, shiny sweat from his scalp showing through his hair. He walked back into the house, seeming relieved to get away from me.

I caught my breath and admitted to my wife that as I'd told him the story I felt as if I were making a confession. She seemed to understand that, though I don't know how. She asked if I still wanted to meet our friends for dinner. I said that I was depleted and needed nutrition to get my motor skills back to normal.

On our way out the front door, the hostess said good-bye and thanked us for coming.

"Did you have a good time?" she asked after looking us over.

"It's been therapeutic," I said.

Water

My wife and I had been around and around about it. Our next-door neighbors, Chuck and Sandra, were crazy about watering their yard. For the past year or so their sprinkler system had run through its cycle at least three times every day of the week. Our lots sloped down toward the property line between the houses and that area was soaked and muddy all the time. The runoff from their sprinklers ran down our sidewalk and along the curb the length of the block and beyond. It also ran under their back fence and down the alley. They'd created a man-made creek that ran constantly through our neighborhood. Mud stained our sidewalk and when I went out to the mailbox, which was alongside theirs at the property line, I couldn't step in the grass nearby without my shoes sinking into it.

Should we phone the city and register a complaint? Should we talk to them or keep our mouths shut? They were friends of ours. We'd been to their house for dinner a couple of times and we'd had them over. We decided that if we wanted to do something about their watering we should talk to them rather than call the city. But we asked ourselves if we should, if it was any of our business. Who were we to tell them to cut down on their watering?

There was a complicating factor. The last time we were at their house for dinner, Sandra told us that someone had put an angry, unsigned note in their mailbox about their Cairn terrier, Champ. Chuck and Sandra had a habit of letting Champ out in their back-yard at five in the morning. He started yapping and didn't stop until they brought him inside an hour and a half later. We knew they kept Champ shut in their utility room all day while they were at work. His trip to the backyard was his main breath of air for the day, and when they let him out he went nuts.

Sandra asked if we ever heard Champ barking in the mornings. We admitted that he sometimes woke us up and that it was hard to go back to sleep when he did. Chuck sat quietly sipping vodka as he let this information soak in. A pause hung in the air. We both told them we didn't write the note, but we weren't sure they believed it. We'd complained to them about the people who lived on the other side of us. The kids screamed and played loud music at their swimming pool for hours. The father sat at poolside smoking a lengthy cigar and yelling at the kids and into the house at his wife. We'd retaliated by opening our back door and playing Frank Sinatra turned way up. The neighbors toned down their music, but most of the screaming and all of the cigar smoking continued. Our stories about them could have made Chuck and Sandra consider the idea that one or both of us wrote the note.

Sandra unfolded the note and handed it to us, and she watched us as our eyes scanned its block letters. It said that by letting Champ out so early, Chuck and Sandra were making him a menace to the neighborhood, waking up everyone within earshot long before sunrise, ruining people's workdays, jangling their nerves, subjecting them to daily torment with no consideration for anything but their dog's need to clear his bowels and bark at fence posts. When we gave the note back to Sandra, she told us they'd decided to wait until later in the morning to let out Champ.

Elaine and I figured that if we said anything about their watering, they'd connect it with the note in their mailbox. They'd get mad at us and stay mad and we'd have to live with their anger. So we kept quiet and watched them water. Even when we had several days and nights of rain the watering continued. They'd water right through a thunderstorm, and almost anytime we watered they'd turn on their system for an extra run through.

One night close to midnight we heard their water come on as we lay in bed reading.

"Isn't that the fourth time today?" I asked.

"We need to start keeping a log."

"This morning they soaked the newspaper. The water ran inside the plastic bag."

"I've had it," Elaine said. "I'm sayonarring." She turned off her lamp and rolled over. "I need somebody to hug me. But don't twitch around."

I shut off my light and moved against her. But I couldn't stop twitching and I soon rolled away so she could get to sleep.

The next evening I noticed an unusual amount of water running down our sidewalk from the direction of Chuck and Sandra's house. Their sprinklers weren't on at the time. I went out for a look and as soon as I opened the door I heard running water. I walked across the yard, and when I neared the property line my feet started to sink in the turf. On the side of their house, I saw water pouring through the drain-off pipe for their air conditioning system.

I went back inside and told Elaine. We talked about it and agreed that I should call them. I'd probably get their recorder, and I could say something in the message about water constantly running between our houses.

Their recorder came on after six or eight rings. I told them that gallons of water were pouring from the pipe on the side of their house. I said I'd noticed an almost continuous flow of water between our houses from the watering they did, but today was more than usual and they might want to check into it. Before the flow from the pipe started, had they noticed the mud on the sidewalk, the runoff in the street and alley, and the standing water?

Excess watering might damage their grass and attract termites and mosquitoes. The newspaper had been running articles about disease-ridden mosquitoes being attracted to standing water. Elaine leaned in and whispered to stop. I told them I hoped everything was okay with them and that the overflow problem with the pipe was nothing serious and hung up.

"Too much?"

"You were getting carried away, but maybe they'll knock it off."

Chuck called back in less than an hour, and I picked up.

"Tommy, thanks for letting us know about the pipe. We've had that problem before and we need to get it looked at. I've made an appointment with a repairman, so that water source should be stopping soon. But about the other thing. You're saying you want to see me water less."

"You water three times a day. I water twice a week and that seems to take care of it."

"And this has exactly what to do with you?"

"It wastes water. It gets mud on our sidewalk, and our yard on your side is soggy. You water while it's raining and that makes no sense. I don't know how you can justify watering three times a day even when it rains two or three days straight."

"It sounds like my watering bothers you quite a bit, Tommy. And that note about Champ. You said you didn't write it. Isn't that what you said?"

"We didn't write the note. Neither of us did."

"Does it occur to you that I pay for every bit of the water I use? Does it occur to you that I won't drain the lakes dry with my watering? Lots of rain lately, you said so yourself. Did that occur to you?"

"You're wasting water."

"Well let's just see what happens."

He hung up.

His watering increased to five times a day for two weeks. Then he went back to three times a day. Soon after that, Chuck again began to let Champ out in the yard at five in the morning. Champ's yapping seemed more vigorous and relentless than before, and I imagined Chuck in the yard provoking him.

About a week later I heard Chuck's voice shouting into our recorder. He said he could see our lights on and he wasn't going to hang up until I came to the phone. We were eating dinner, but I put down my fork and took the call.

Another note had turned up in their mailbox. Again the note was unsigned, but Chuck told me he knew I'd written it. He said it had the same printing as the previous note and he took that as confirmation that I'd written the first one. He read it to me. The note asked what motivated him to torment his neighbors with such malice. It said he'd obviously gotten the other message and had some understanding of the complaint, but he'd sat around in his den drinking vodka and working himself into a frenzy of self-righteousness. No one could tell him what to do with his dog, he probably muttered drunkenly to himself. He could hang it upside down from a tree and leave it there if he wanted to. He and Sandra should be reported to an animal rights organization for shutting Champ in their utility room while they were at work. Every moment Champ spent loose in the yard he expressed a wail of torment. Imagine the knotty feelings of abandonment Champ had to deal with as he ran back and forth for hours in that tiny utility room. On the other hand, maybe the dog was upset by all the wasted water that Chuck ran under the fence. Perhaps he lived in horror that he would be slurped under the muddy bog that Chuck had created in his backyard. Was he trying to create Lake Chuck around his house? The note writer speculated that Champ may have developed a fear of water. Did he leave muddy footprints around the house? Did Chuck punish him for putting his muddy paws on the carpet?

Chuck was almost delirious with rage by the time he finished reading. Elaine could hear him shouting into the phone. I wanted to interrupt him, but I knew he wouldn't stop until he'd gotten to the end.

"I didn't write the note," I said. "Not that one or the first one."

"At least have the decency to admit it," Chuck said. "All this about the water and the utility room? How many people know about the utility room?"

"Maybe a lot of people."

"I don't like the implied threats, Tommy. Champ hanging upside down from a tree? Don't talk about torturing my dog. Don't come at me with your Lake Chuck cracks. How many people hate me as much as you do about this watering?"

"It's hundreds of gallons of water down the drain. I understand why this person is fed up with you. You've got no business calling me up and yelling down my throat when anyone on the block could have written those notes. It makes me angry that you don't care about waking the neighbors and that you enjoy causing us the trouble. Shut up and look in the mirror, Chuck. You're not the victim and we don't all have to sit quietly and accept what you want."

I hung up on him. I went to the front of the house and looked out the window to see if he would charge out his door and come toward the house. If he did, I was going out and meeting him halfway. He'd be down to his neck in mud if I got the jump on him. Elaine came after me, grabbing me by the shoulder.

"Don't go out there. Let it settle down."

"He's not going to settle down anytime soon."

"Let's just stay out of his way."

I stood at the window watching. I saw a big snake slither from Chuck's yard onto the sidewalk. Chuck didn't come out.

After his call we noticed that we stopped hearing Champ in the mornings. Another week went by and Chuck turned off his sprinklers. When we were getting ready for bed one night Elaine mentioned that she couldn't remember the last time she'd heard a peep out of Champ. I couldn't remember hearing Champ since getting the call from Chuck. In addition to the early-morning barking, we used to hear him yap on weekends, and he often went into a frenzy when I went out to put the garbage in the bin.

For that matter we hadn't seen Chuck or Sandra, except early on a Sunday morning when Elaine happened to see Chuck come out in his bathrobe and pull an armload of mail from his box. His hair was dirty and he needed a shave.

Elaine wanted to call their other next-door neighbors, Pam and Don, who sometimes socialized with them. I preferred to stay off the radar, especially since things were dry and quiet.

"I just want to see if they've heard anything," Elaine said. "Chuck could be calling people and flying off at them about the notes. Maybe someone admitted it. Then we'd be off the hook."

I went into my study rather than listen, but I could hear Elaine talking and laughing. The call kept going and going.

"It's safe," Elaine shouted when it was finally over. I emerged and sat down with her at the kitchen table.

"Pam knew about the notes," Elaine said. "She told me Chuck still thinks you wrote them, maybe with help from me. Pam thinks Don could have written the notes, but he won't admit it. She says he didn't want to tell Chuck in person how annoyed they were by all the barking and watering. Anyway, somebody called the city. The city contacted Chuck and told him he'd been using extravagant amounts of water. They issued him a warning and that's why he stopped. He thinks you're the one who turned him in, but Pam thinks Don might have made the call and won't tell her because he thinks it's better if she doesn't know. She says he thinks it's better if she doesn't know a lot of things, but that's another story. Champ is still around. They let him out in the yard to relieve himself and then take him back in. Chuck is pouring large quantities of vodka down his throat. Pam thinks it's a substitute for pouring so much water into his yard. When she said that, I wondered if she could have written the notes herself."

As we spoke, Chuck's water came on.

"Can he hear us?" I asked.

"If he could hear us he'd know we didn't write the notes."

I listened to the water running.

"You didn't, did you?" Elaine asked.

"Did you?"

The
Dangerous
Couple

I didn't like her. We saw her and her husband at parties given by some people we knew who entertained a lot, and at one of the parties, while my wife was off talking to someone in the next room, she told me that her husband was impotent. It wasn't that I'd asked her or that we were engaged in some deep conversation or that she knew me well enough to tell me such things. She happened to be standing next to me and was watching him across the room and she came out with it. There were other reasons I didn't like her. She had a smirk that never let up, and she rarely showed any interest in what anyone said.

I didn't like her husband either. An overbearing one-upper, knew a better vodka than you were drinking, a better car than you were driving, knew more than you did about any subject that came up. Too much domination in his voice, wanted to be the only voice in the room, talked over you if you tried to get a word in, gobbled you up like food.

I didn't like them separately, and I liked them even less together. When they were together she would eel herself against his body, her hands moving over his torso, her eyes searching her surroundings for other visceral stimulation. He held a martini in one hand while his other hand wandered over her from behind, and his eyes roamed hungrily around the room as if somehow connected to the tour of his hand. They were like two people masturbating publicly and in unison.

I wouldn't mention either one of them, but something happened that I can't put to rest. My wife and I were at a restaurant one night, a small restaurant, dark and romantic, secluded booths, lots of angles, known for its wine list and its veal, and we saw him there with another woman. I could see them clearly and my wife could too if she looked back, though there were tables and booths between our booth and theirs. He would have had to turn and look over his shoulder to see us. The woman had a view of us but did not know us, and I could watch everything without drawing their attention, only my wife had to turn her head to watch. But there was no need for her to turn her head because I filled her in on what was going on. I told her they were drinking martinis, made with the greatest vodka in the world, no doubt, I could imagine him ordering it for her, the only way to drink a martini, the exact number of olives, the exact amount of vermouth. I told her about his hand winding around the mystery guest's hand, how they leaned in and whispered and gazed into each other's faces, his other hand dropping under the table for field trips up and down her legs. Finally my wife told me to shut up, she couldn't stand to listen to me anymore, it was none of our business. I shut up but kept watching, thinking that we already had an invitation to the people's house where we usually saw him, and I looked forward to finding out if he and his wife would be there again together.

When we arrived at the party I saw them at once, he with his martini in hand, she with him in hand, he talking with another couple, keeping them informed on some important topic, she showing no interest in whatever that topic was, her eyes casting about the room greedily for something to light on. Her eyes passed over us as if we were invisible, no sense of familiarity at all, and as we moved into the room and began greeting people she split away from her husband and wound through the guests toward a food table. It was then that I went toward her, no conscious plan, moving on impulse, but an impulse that had been gathering wind, I could remember seeing myself go toward her in the back of my mind.

I said her name, the first time I had ever said it to her. She was facing the table, and she turned and looked me over, something in the sound of my voice made her curious. I watched her face, her smirk, and she watched my eyes taking her in and my eyes made her more curious.

"I ran into your husband at a restaurant."

"He didn't tell me."

"He didn't see me."

"You didn't say hello?"

"I didn't say hello because he was busy."

"What was he busy doing?"

"He was busy drinking martinis with another woman. He didn't look impotent when I saw him so I didn't think I should interrupt."

The smirk broadened, her mouth opened. Her color heightened and my heart thrust against my chest. Her eye teeth were long and pointed, and her eyes were all over my face. I had the feeling that her clothes would fall off her onto the floor, and my mind filled with images of her body winding around me, her arms raised above her head. She moved close to me, and I heard her tongue move inside her mouth.

"He can respond if the situation is just right," she said. "I know what he does. He tells me and I want to hear it. Did you think I'd be surprised? I am surprised you told me. I'm interested in that."

I kept looking at her mouth, her eye teeth, the darkness down her throat.

"If you want to tell me more about it, we can leave the room," she said and laughed. "Do you want to leave the room with me? You want to touch me? But if it's not okay for him why should it be okay for you? I don't mean I care if you're a hypocrite, I'm just worried about you. You may be in over your head, can't let the animal loose. On the other hand, you can't stop looking at me. Can I do anything to help you relax? My blood won't be racing in ten minutes unless you strike."

I said nothing, denied nothing.

"Let me know," she said. "I enjoyed our chat."

I didn't watch her walk away. I leaned on the food table with both hands and closed my eyes for a moment. I heard for the first time how noisy it was in the room, the noise roared inside me though a minute before I had hardly noticed it. I gathered myself and turned, hoping my wife would not be watching, hoping I'd been shielded by the other guests. But she was watching, and standing next to her was the martini-drinker's wife herself, the two of them talking and looking right at me. I couldn't find the nerve to go toward them and couldn't let myself think what they might be talking about. Was she telling my wife what I'd said to her and how we'd both reacted? Was she proposing that my wife leave the room with us? Trying not to seem in too big a hurry, I made my way toward a pair of open French doors that led out into a garden. Outside I breathed in the air and tried to clear my head, but my head would not clear, and I imagined her husband approaching me and warning me to be careful with his wife, she'd put me between two pieces of bread and that would be the end of me. Then I felt a hand on my shoulder and I started.

"It's just me," my wife said and took away her hand. She watched my face as she spoke. "I saw you go right to her when we came in. I wondered if you were telling her what you saw. It was the only thing I could think of that you could be telling her, but I couldn't believe you'd do it. She said it wasn't news to her."

I shook my head.

"She also said we shouldn't worry about her," she went on. "She knows who she's married to and her husband knows who he's married to. She looked at me with her smile when she said that, the side of her mouth up, and then she looked at you. You turned around after holding yourself up with the table, and when you saw us together I thought you would fall over backwards. You fled."

But I was not safe. Looking over her shoulder I saw the husband emerge through the doorway, a fresh martini in hand.

"I hear I'm being investigated," he said, laughing.

He introduced himself. We'd been introduced several times before, but he either didn't remember or assumed we'd forgotten. He addressed me with a name that was not my name but had the same first letter as my name.

"I appreciate you looking after my wife," he said, "and she has assured me that she understands why you took it upon yourself to tell her what you told her, even though you had never spoken to her for more than a few minutes before tonight, is that correct?"

I nodded.

"But I do not share her understanding of whatever purpose you had in mind. I'm curious what you were looking for and I've asked her, but she says it's not up to her to explain. Can you tell me what it is that she understands?"

I didn't answer, and if I had wanted to answer I have no idea what I would have said.

"I am sure she told you that we have no secrets in our marriage, maybe a few, but not on this subject," he continued. "But you didn't know that when you told her, and you didn't know much of anything else about her when you told her, and I can believe that you could never have foreseen that you would reach her the way you did. I've seen that look in her eye before, as you can probably imagine, and I know when the pot's been stirred. Your wife should be aware that you are on the loose stirring pots, and she should also be aware that your pot's been stirred. It's only right, don't you agree, that she should know what her husband has been up to."

He paused and sipped his drink. My wife looked ahead at neither of us.

"You're lucky to come out of this as well as you did," he added. "Other people might not be as understanding as we are, others might feel they owed you some physical damage to get even with you. I suggest you think about what caused you to behave so recklessly and beyond reason. For your own safety you should have some awareness of where your urges might lead you in the future. In the meantime, I want you to know how much my wife appreciates your interest in her. I don't know when she's had such fun. Good luck with him," he said to my wife and took a step toward her and kissed her on the cheek.

Then he nodded to me and to her and left.

"Are you ready to go?" she asked me.

We went back through the house and out the front door and spoke to no one, looked at no one.

We didn't talk about it as we drove home or as we lay awake in the middle of the night. I feared she would start in on me and ask me things. My voice seemed trapped in my throat, images of the couple silenced me. I kept seeing them standing together at a party, her body against his, their eyes roving, she squeezing my severed tongue in her hand, he raising his martini to me and winking.

Shake

I was having a discussion with the woman I'd been seeing. Not exactly a discussion. We were on the floor in her den. I was on top of her. We did say a thing or two. We were well along the way but not about to finish. I was unaware of my surroundings. To my surprise, she was not unaware. She saw something. Her head popped up over my shoulder, pushing my head back. She pointed at the window over her kitchen table and chairs. I looked back where she pointed. A boy's face. He'd been watching. He saw us see him and he took off toward the alley.

I reacted. I started to get up. She pulled me back down.

"Let him go," she said.

"I'm not letting him go. This is none of his business."

I pulled away from her. I grabbed my pants and shirt and started putting them on.

"He's already gone," she said. "What will you do if you find him?"

"He's in trouble. Let's just say that."

"Don't hurt him. He didn't do anything."

"I call it doing something."

I jammed my feet in my shoes.

"Don't hurt that boy," she shouted at me as I left.

I ran out the back door and around the corner to where my car was parked. I stuck the key in and started it up. I drove slowly around the neighborhood and looked between the houses for him, thinking he might be perched in front of another window. I planned to get out and chase him. He couldn't outrun me. He was too little and wasn't strong enough. I'd grab him and lift him up, look in his face, tell him a few things he'd take with him. He wouldn't forget what I told him or the look on my face. I'd make sure he remembered.

I'd done the same thing when I was little. Not at someone else's place but where I lived with my father. My mother was away. I heard the noise inside the bedroom and wondered. I quietly pushed the door open. My father's pants and shirt were on the floor and he was on top of a woman who wasn't my mother. I didn't know what they were doing, but it made me feel sick to watch.

She saw me and pointed. I saw him pull the plug out. He came after me, sticking out, bouncing. I ran but couldn't get away from him.

"Don't tell your mother," he said when he grabbed me and lifted me.

He stank. The wet hair on his chest stank and his armpits stank. His face was damp. He could feel me shaking.

"You got me?" he asked in my face.

Since he was telling me not to tell her, I knew she'd want to know.

"She's no different than I am. Believe me."

He put me down then. It was right in my face, pointing at me. My face was burning.

"Deal?" he asked but didn't offer his hand. To him, it was a deal whether we shook on it or not.

He went back in the room with the woman. He closed the door. I heard him prop something against it. He said something and I heard the woman laugh.

I turned a corner and saw him walking down the street, left side. His back was to me. He wore a dirty gray T-shirt. Hair cut down to his scalp, like a grown man who's balding. Like me. He walked with his head down, not looking ahead or around. He didn't hear me behind him and it gave him a jolt when I rolled up next to him and ran the window down. He stopped and looked at me. I stayed in the car. It wasn't the way I planned. I saw him shaking, but he didn't run this time. Maybe he figured he couldn't get away or maybe he was waiting to see if I got out of my car before he ran.

"You saw us," I said.

He nodded.

"How long?"

He shrugged.

"Five minutes?"

He shook his head.

"Less?"

He didn't answer.

"You go around looking in people's windows?"

He didn't answer.

"You won't tell anybody what you saw?"

He shook his head.

"You know what you were looking at?"

He nodded.

"It would embarrass her. You understand that?"

He nodded.

"I never told," I said. "Never."

He looked at me and waited, his face red.

"I'm telling you. I saw them. I never told her. I couldn't. What would have happened if I had? To me and to them. Think about that. What would happen? Would it help you? Would it help anything? Keep it to yourself. That's what I'm saying."

He nodded, still shaking.

"Inside your head. That's where you should keep it. Keep it there. You'll learn to do that. You have to."

He waited.

"Don't go back there. Don't look in her window. What's inside people's windows is not your business. You never know who or what you'll be looking at. You follow me?"

He nodded.

"Do you?"

He nodded again.

I saw a couple on foot turn the corner ahead and come toward us. I ran my window up.

I waved at the boy. He didn't wave. I waved again. He waved.

I left him there. As I drove away I watched him in my rearview mirror. The couple walked past him.

I went back to her. She'd dressed. We sat on the sofa in her den.

"You found him?"

She could tell by looking at me.

"Did you hurt him?"

"I didn't get out of the car. We had a discussion."

"Did you scare him?"

"I talked to him. He won't come back."

"I don't want him talking to the neighbors."

"You told me not to go after him."

"I was afraid you'd hurt him."

"He won't talk."

"You're sure? What did you say?"

"I told him a story."

"What story? Was it true?"

I nodded.

"What was it?"

"Between him and me."

"You know this kid?"

"Not before."

She leaned against me. She stopped talking. The silence was between us. We were there in it.

The Neighbor

Down the front walk for the paper, hair askew, mouth webby, sweatsuit and slippers, windy but not too cold, Saturday, end of February. Next-door neighbor also out for the paper, picks it up, looks at me, pauses, waves me toward him. Seen the guy but never said more than a few words to him, lived side by side for three years, big hairy guy, T-shirt and plaid robe. I go over and say hello, shake hands, huge hand, hair up the sleeve under his robe, down his unshaven face into his T-shirt, deep cleft in his chin, glazed blue eyes that stare at me. "I want to tell you something, got a minute?" he asks, arm around my back, walking up the path with me. "Coffee's on," he says. "It's about this guy. I've got to tell somebody."

My wife's visiting her sister out of town so she won't miss me, my coffee's not on, my door's unlocked but no one knows it. I decide to go with him. He opens his front door and waves me inside and I follow the direction of his hand. Lives alone, travels a lot on business, clean place, quiet, no TV or radio on, sun coming through the back window into his den, which is where we go. He tells me to have a seat, his hand pointing toward the sofa, and I sit down, looking around at nothing in particular, while he goes for the coffee. Bookshelves more or less empty, walls blank except for an old black and white picture of a couple who could be his parents. Back with our coffee he hands me mine and sits in a worn leather chair he must have had at least twenty years, sips from his mug and then lowers it.

"A man is married to a woman he loves and leads a decent life, no noticeable harm to others, but slowly he becomes obsessed with the idea that he should not have children. It is the time of their lives when they would be having them, his wife wants them and talks to him about it, but he will not agree to have any. Her parents ask if they plan to start a family, his parents ask, he's an only child and his father wants him to carry on the family name, the clock is ticking, but something inside him stops it. He tries to change his own mind and listens to his wife when she tries to change it. He asks himself what voice is speaking in him telling him it is a bad idea. He does not know the voice, does not associate the voice with himself or with anything in his childhood or family life growing up. But he knows that it is not someone else's voice, he does not think he is inhabited, and he listens and looks inward and tries to connect himself with the voice."

He sips his coffee and gazes at me and then goes on.

"Gradually his sense of himself changes. When he showers he begins to feel that he is washing off an animal smell and when he eats he feels the urge to pick up his food with his hands. He begins to have dreams in which he fathers children with furry bodies and tails. He is tormented by unrestrained sexual fantasies and by what goes through his mind when he makes love to his wife and by the sight of blood on the walls when he is angry. He questions whether he was ever the person he once thought he was and thinks that he could never responsibly consider having children and never share with anyone his reasons for not wanting them. He feels that he must hide his underlife from others and sympathizes with his wife for being stuck with him. Once in the middle of the night he finds himself weeping loud enough that he wakes her up. She turns on her light and holds him, but the comfort she offers makes him feel worse. As he sees it he does not deserve to be comforted. He fears that she will ask him why he is weeping, but she does not ask, does not want to further upset him, he imagines, and her consideration of his state of mind further upsets him. He asks her to turn off the light and promises to go back to sleep and be quiet. She does as he asks and he breathes deeply and relaxes enough to stop crying.

"The next day she looks at him with worry when he leaves for work and all that day he sees her image as she looked at him. When he returns she says she'd like to have a talk, and they sit at the kitchen table and she tells him that she wants him to think again about having children. She says that children could add something to his life, could give him someone outside himself and her to care about and love. They would be part of him, he would see his face in their faces, and his blood and hers would flow together inside them. He would probably see in them parts of his parents he had never noticed were there. He wants to tell her to stop, he has heard all of it before, but she is trying to help him so he listens.

"After she finishes she waits for him to answer, but he does not say anything. He restrains himself from shouting at her and knows that if he speaks, his voice will reveal what he feels, no matter how tactfully he chooses his words. He wants to ask her what he imagines he would turn the poor things into, but he does not, she would not understand the question because she does not know him the way he knows himself. He stares at his wife, and his silence and the look on his face stay with her. She leaves him at the kitchen table, and after that she is never the same with him. The distance between them grows and he never again touches her and imagines that she wouldn't want him to. He believes that she'd be better off without him and has no trouble convincing himself of this idea, though he cannot persuade himself to leave her. He neglects her and sees his neglect as in her best interest, as his way of leading her to seek a different life. She endures him longer than he thought she could bear it, but finally tells him she wants him to leave. He moves out and lives in a hotel for a few weeks, and then moves into a house.

"She is kind in the divorce, which is not surprising to him, she is that type of person. He still loves her, but out of consideration for her he does not say it. He hates himself for losing her but resigns himself to the idea that he cannot get her back. He feels relieved that the pressure to have children is over, despite the price of his relief, but he often asks himself what drove him, how he got where he is. He asks himself what he would say if he told his own story. He can imagine telling what happened but not how it happened. He becomes preoccupied with the idea of telling his story to someone, but he is alone and at a loss who to tell it to. He considers going to a therapist and spilling his guts for a fee, but he never acts on the idea. He doesn't want a prescription and he doesn't want a professional contact but a human contact, he wants to tell his story one person to another. The idea of telling it to his ex-wife keeps recurring to him, but he knows that she's had enough of him already. What can he expect her to do for him anyway? She might think he is getting around to asking her to take him back and that idea humiliates him and holds him away from her, though his urge to speak to her as honestly as he can is not silenced. Sometimes he tries to imagine that a willing listener is in his house, but he can never surrender himself to the fantasy, can never imagine who the listener could be. He writes as much of his story as he can on legal pads, but reading through these pages he sees no common thread that could be used to make sense of him. At times he goes over the pages and tries to make additions, but the process leads nowhere. Years of silence pass and he rattles around in his house with his story trapped inside him."

He stands and asks if I want more coffee. I tell him I've had enough and hand him my mug as he walks past, relieved to have a break to gather my thoughts. Questions roll through my mind. Where did the story come from, why tell it to me, what will I say about it, who is the story about, is the story about me? Has he talked to my wife, did he meet my old school friend when traveling, did my friend tell the story he heard from me and who it was about? How unlikely a coincidence would that be, and how unlikely that he would tell a story so much like me without meaning to? Not the same story, embellished and exaggerated compared to mine, but similar. Still married, wife who wants children away in anger, marriage coming apart. He comes back with his coffee, sits in his leather chair, and as I watch him take a drink of it I imagine people ransacking my house, opening drawers and dumping their contents, looking under furniture and up in the attic for something they cannot find.

"I heard the story in a hotel bar, though most of the time I avoid talking to anyone in bars and just go in for one drink, throw it down and then leave. But in this case an unshaven man approached me and started talking and would not let me go until he was finished. He said that a friend of his had told him the story and that it was about his friend, but the insistent way he told it made me suspect that it was about him. You and I live next door to each other and have never met. When we see each other picking up the mail or the newspaper we say hello and maybe comment on the weather. I sometimes ask myself what I could say to you, or the neighbor on the other side, that might begin a conversation, and when I saw you I decided to tell you this story. I hope you don't mind. I wanted to tell the story but have no one at hand to tell it to. I have lived alone for years now. I have no children and my wife divorced me. Somewhere I lost touch with people, my inner life became separate from others. Maybe you are unlucky, maybe you would rather be at home reading your paper, but by chance you walked out the door the same time I did."

Then I spoke. "Or you may have sat at your window waiting until I came out for my paper. Maybe when you saw me you walked out the door and then waved me over and took me under your arm. You must know that I have no children and you may know that my wife has not been with me for more than a week. You may have heard us arguing or seen us through a window shouting at each other, and maybe you've talked with her and she's told you that I don't want children."

"I haven't talked to your wife and I've never heard you argue. I didn't know the story would have anything to do with your life."

"I don't know you. I have no way of sorting out the story you've told me or why you decided to tell it. I don't know what to believe. For all I know you talk to my wife on a regular basis while I'm at work. When you're not out of town you may sit for hours with her, drinking coffee and listening to her pour out her heart. It does seem strange that almost your first words to me are this story about a supposedly unknown couple's intimate lives."

"You're right, the story is too intimate, and you would have to know more about me to understand why I am telling it. I suppose I wanted you to listen and understand without my telling you. I protected myself by not being direct, which did not help your understanding. The story is about me. You are the only person I have told it to, for years it has seemed too much to get out, too much for anyone but someone close to hear. You are close, you are next door. I did not sit at the window and wait for you, I saw you and asked you inside to listen because you were there."

He leans back, face slack, a look of uneasiness. He does not want me in his house any longer and I don't want to be around him either. I get up to go.

"Don't tell anyone the story," he says, not looking at me.

I look at him and wonder. Is the story really about him? What could he be up to? Does he know why he is telling it to me? What does he want me to understand? Which story is it that he doesn't want me to tell? I want to answer him, but I can think of no way to begin.

How
Tommy Lee
Turned Out
Abnormal

In a way the change in Stuart came on all of a
sudden and in a way it had been building up slowly for some time.
Stuart had had a problem with our son Tommy Lee ever since
the boy started growing into a man. There it was, the first hair
on Tommy Lee's chin and Stuart was eyeing it with the first in-
kling of worry. And he changed more as Tommy Lee changed, as
Tommy Lee's voice got deeper, as his legs got longer and more hair
grew out of his face.

"What is it with you?" I finally broke down and asked Stuart
after watching this go on.

He just shrugged, but I could see that there was more.

"You've been fretting over something to do with Tommy Lee. Has he done something?"

"Nothing that I know of," Stuart glanced at me and said, not denying the gist of what I was saying.

He sat down in the bedroom chair and put his head in his hands. I'd always known Stuart had his moods, but this was worse.

"So there is something going on then," I said.

Stuart didn't answer but dropped his hands from his face and opened his eyes wide and blinked as if he were just waking up from a troubling dream.

But he didn't wake up.

A few nights after that I noticed that Stuart kept staring at Tommy Lee over dinner, and I began staring at Tommy Lee to see if I could figure out what Stuart was looking at.

"Why are you looking at him?" Stuart asked me, putting a forkful of pork chop in his mouth and chewing it.

"Me?" I answered. "You're the one who's looking at him. I was trying to see what you were looking at."

Stuart squinted at me, why I didn't know. I leaned back in my chair, away from Stuart's squint.

"What did you see?" he asked then.

"Tommy Lee," I told him.

"What else?"

"He needs a shave."

Stuart gave Tommy Lee's stubble a look. Then he rubbed his own face.

"So he does," Stuart agreed. He seemed fixated on the sight of the hair on Tommy Lee's face. "Once it starts growing," Stuart said strangely, "you can't make it stop."

Tommy Lee changed colors and looked at me, not knowing what to think of his father.

"What are you looking over there for?" Stuart asked him. "You expect her to answer for you?"

"Answer for what?" Tommy Lee wanted to know, and so did I.

Stuart just sneered to himself as if he'd expected Tommy Lee to play dummy, and I threw my wadded paper napkin—which I'd been wringing in my hands—down on the table.

"What in the world is happening to you?" I asked Stuart.

"Don't turn this around toward me, your royal highness, the queen of the dinner table."

I'd heard a few choice words from Stuart before, but he'd never called me that one. "Where did you breathe the thin air this argument came from?" I said.

Tommy Lee's mouth hung open, tiny hairs standing on end on his upper lip and sticking out from the bottom of his chin.

"We're all breathing it, Doreen," Stuart answered.

"I'm not breathing the same air you're breathing. Not at this moment I'm not."

"Get up and shave that hair off your face, Tommy Lee," Stuart shouted. "I won't look at that hairy face while I'm eating."

Then Stuart jerked himself to his feet, his legs jarring the table, splattering gravy from his plate and setting off a clatter of dishes, his chair almost tipping over backwards. Tommy Lee's eyes followed him as he flung himself out of the room.

"He sure wants me to shave," Tommy Lee said.

"He's flipped off to a different channel than we're watching," I told him.

Was Stuart remorseful after this strange episode? No. That night in bed, thirty minutes after the lights were out, his angry, raving voice popped my eyelids open:

"He thinks he's a man. He thinks he can replace me. Is that what he thinks?"

I squirmed out of bed, snapping at him in the dark:

"It must be the change of life you're going through, Stuart."

"Well we both know there's a change in Tommy Lee."

"You want to turn him around backwards and keep him moving till he's back inside my womb again?"

"Why did you say that?" Stuart sat up and yelled.

"What?"

"Back inside your womb."

Tommy Lee's door opened. I heard his feet moving toward us and a moment later our door opened. He switched on the light and looked in at us, narrowing his eyes from the glare, his hair in chaotic, upright tufts. He stood there in his wrinkled pajamas, still half asleep.

"Is the place on fire?" he asked us.

"It might as well be," Stuart shot back at him.

Tommy Lee looked at me for an answer to his father's riddle. His eyes were cloudy.

"Your father's mind is on fire, Tommy Lee," I said.

"So you're a team now," Stuart accused us, "and I'm on the outside looking in."

"We're not a team," I said.

"What's he doing in here then? He seems to be running to your defense."

"Defense?" Tommy Lee said. "Is he doing something to you, Mama?"

"Am I doing something to you, Doreen?" Stuart asked. "Can he rush in here and throw himself between us?"

"This is all in your imagination," I told Stuart.

"Don't try to calm me down," he answered me. "And don't expect me to roll over and die just to get out of your way, Tommy Lee. It's you against me now."

Tommy Lee gazed at his father, his mouth opening and his lips starting to move as he struggled to comprehend.

"What's happened to him, Mama?" he asked. "What is he talking about?"

"You can talk to me, Tommy Lee. I'm still here and I'm still your dad," Stuart said, poking himself in the chest as he said the last word, his voice cracking.

Tommy Lee went to Stuart then and leaned over to hug him, but Stuart put his arms up between them.

"I'm sorry it's come to this, son," Stuart said. "This is not the way I wanted it, but let's not pretend."

"It's not the way I want it either, Daddy," Tommy Lee said to him.

I drew in a deep breath, shivering with nerves.

"I swear I don't know who I'm in bed with anymore," I said.

"You're in bed with me, that's who," Stuart asserted.

"But who are you?" I asked. "That's what I don't know."

"And therefore?"

"Therefore I'm not climbing back in bed with you."

"And you say this is all my imagination."

"I still say it."

"If you leave my bed where do you plan to go?" Stuart asked.

"To the sofa," I told him.

"I'll take the sofa, Mama," Tommy Lee said. "You can stay in my bed."

"Did I hear what he just said," Stuart asked, "or was that just my imagination?"

"He's trying to help me, Stuart."

"To help you get away from me."

"I'll stay on the sofa, Tommy Lee," I said. "Your father would go off on a rampage if I slept in your bed."

"Don't condescend to me, Doreen," Stuart said. "Come out with it. You want to be in the boy's bed."

"It beats the sofa, Stuart," I told him. "Wouldn't you rather sleep in a bed than on a sofa?"

"I'd rather sleep in my bed than on a sofa and you wouldn't."

"I'd rather stay on the sofa tonight than in your bed and I'd rather be in Tommy Lee's bed, since he offered it to me, than on the sofa. Are you satisfied?"

"This is not about satisfying me. I'm not satisfied. My wife is leaving my bed. Am I supposed to be the one who's satisfied?"

"I'm tired of this," I said. "I'm going to bed."

"And where would you rather sleep, Tommy Lee?" Stuart asked then.

"I'll go to the sofa," Tommy Lee said.

"But wouldn't you rather sleep in your own bed than on the sofa? You were sleeping in your bed before your mother moved in with you and you've never slept on the sofa before."

"She can have the bed," Tommy Lee said, at a loss.

"You're afraid I'd object if you slept with my wife," Stuart said.

Tommy Lee went pale, his mind a whirl of anxiety and confusion. He cast about for something to say.

"I'll just sleep on the sofa," he got out.

"So you can protect me from the truth?" Stuart asked loudly. "So you can protect yourself from the truth, Tommy Lee?"

Tommy Lee didn't even try to answer him. He sighed heavily and sank inside his skin and squeezed his head in his hands.

"Get off his back, Stuart," I shouted. "He offered me his bed to try to be nice. Someone has to be nice around here because you're making the place unlivable. I can't live this way and neither can Tommy Lee."

"That right, Tommy Lee?"

Tommy Lee waved his hands in the air, then pressed his palms flat down on top of his head as if to keep something from exploding out of it.

"And therefore?" Stuart asked me.

"You're the one who's the menace, Stuart."

"You want me out then, is that it, Doreen?"

"Until you return to the planet I want you out."

"Well, you can't always have what you want," he yelled.

"This conversation is over," I declared. "Tommy Lee, take the sofa. I'll pull down some sheets for you."

He turned at once and headed that way.

"I won't sleep," Stuart warned me. "I'll keep one eye open. I'll know if anything starts to happen. And if it does, I won't let it."

He was leaning toward me, his face distorted, bulging, determined. I shut the bedroom door to block the sight of him.

I set Tommy Lee up on the sofa and then went to bed. I was fed up with Stuart and completely exhausted, and I dropped off to sleep and dropped deep. But before long I was woken up and the sounds of struggle I heard jolted through my nervous system.

"Stuart!" I shouted, my mind suddenly in an uproar.

But he didn't answer. I sat up in bed, listening, afraid, and then I heard the sound of what could have been Tommy Lee struggling to call out to me through a gag. I hopped up into the darkness and grabbed around for the doorknob.

"Stuart, what are you doing to him?"

I found the knob and jerked the door wide and ran to our bedroom for the gun. I switched the light on and rushed to Stuart's side of the bed, but the gun was not in the drawer of his nightstand. By then the sounds had left the house, they were out the back, in the garage, and I ran toward them, hearing Stuart yell at Tommy Lee as he started up the truck.

I got to the door in time to see Stuart backing out of the driveway with Tommy Lee strapped to his seat by the seat belt, his mouth stuffed full of something, tape covering it, the angle of his shoulders and arms telling me that his hands were bound behind him.

I grabbed my keys and went after them.

I knew which way Stuart had to go to reach the blacktop road that led out of the neighborhood and when I reached the road I could see his taillights in the distance to my left, moving fast. I could hardly keep up with him as I followed, and I cursed as his taillights curved out of sight with the bends in the road.

I chased Stuart for nearly half an hour, not knowing for sure if he knew that I was after him, but the way he was driving I figured he did. He ran straight through stop signs and drove way over the speed limit, but he never got away from me. Finally I saw him turn off on a dirt road through a thick wall of trees, and when I reached the road I turned onto it myself and followed him in. The bumpy road forked in several places and I kept losing sight of him. I rolled down the window and listened for the sound of his truck and followed the lead of his dust.

I plunged ahead, screaming at Stuart, the bumps jerking the car up and down, the top of my head jolting against the top of the car. After a while I saw Stuart's truck in a small clearing with ankle-high weeds, his lights off, the doors on both sides hanging open. I could see Stuart on Tommy Lee's side of the truck, Tommy Lee on the ground on his knees, Stuart dragging him ahead with his left hand by a handful of pajama top, brandishing the gun in his free hand. I stopped to the rear of the truck, my headlights like fingers reaching out for them, and threw myself out of the car, stumbling and shouting, the breeze at my back belling out the bottom of my nightgown.

"Let him go, Stuart. What are you doing to him?"

I ran toward them and Stuart turned, shouting back.

"Back up, Doreen. Get out of here. You can't change the truth."

I slowed down, holding my hands up in front of me, and Tommy Lee scrambled to his feet in front of Stuart and tottered and lurched to his right, away from Stuart and the truck.

"What is going on, Stuart? Why did you kidnap Tommy Lee?"

"I don't know," he shouted.

It was all shouting.

"Did you bring him out here to shoot him?"

"I don't know."

"What are you doing here with him?"

He paused, stirring and twisting in his tracks. He pointed his mouth straight up and wailed.

"Do you love me, Doreen?"

"No, I don't, Stuart."

"Do you love Tommy Lee?" he demanded to know, waving the gun toward him.

"Yes, I love Tommy Lee."

"That's what I mean. You love him and not me. You can't change the truth, but it can change you."

He ran toward Tommy Lee and ripped the tape off his mouth and reached in Tommy Lee's mouth and jerked out a sock, which unraveled as it was pulled. Stuart threw that sock back over his head and then grabbed the other sock from Tommy Lee's mouth and flipped it away.

"He told me not to run or he'd shoot me," Tommy Lee cried out first thing.

"Do you love me, Tommy Lee?" Stuart butted in before I could get a word from my mouth.

"I don't know if I do right now, Daddy," Tommy Lee said.

"Do you love your mama?"

"I do. She's the one who's trying to save me."

Stuart shouted, "You see what I'm talking about?" and leaned backwards and fired the gun twice over his head.

"You can't expect him to say he loves you, Stuart, when he doesn't know if you're about to shoot him through the head. You've got his life in your hands."

Stuart groaned and howled and shot the gun toward Tommy Lee, but way over his head, and Tommy Lee ran for it. Stuart yelled for him to stop, firing a warning shot. Tommy Lee flinched, muttering out loud to himself, bolting with his head down for my car, his bound hands splayed and twisting behind him. Stuart watched him flee, and his body suddenly went limp, his arms dropping to his sides. Our eyes met. He raised the gun to his head. I said nothing. He shook his head, then threw the gun in the back of the pickup and ran around the front of the truck to get behind the wheel. I hurried to my car and let in Tommy Lee, who fell sideways into the car, wiggling and squirming to get his feet inside while I reached across his body to shut the door.

I heard Stuart's truck start and I turned my engine over as soon as I could get my hand on the key. The car lurched forward when I put it into gear and I jerked the wheel back toward the road. But Stuart was already ahead of me, and he hit the road at such a clip that all four wheels of his truck left the ground as he pulled up off the roadside onto it. I followed, not knowing what he'd do next, wondering if he would pull his truck across the road to block our path out.

"He's not stopping, Mama," Tommy Lee said.

And the thought that Stuart would simply plunge blindly away from us and not stop until he was far away stunned me, put a chill through me. I kept close enough to see him turn left off the dirt road, heading away from home. I stopped before I turned back onto the road, never considering the idea of chasing after him, but watching his taillights disappear into the night.

Deep Wilderness

BRENT

I was near the end of *Deep Wilderness,* my fifth and best novel, and I was feeling particularly rotten, particularly desperate, and Gail, my wife, was at it again, smoking, as usual, whining, muttering offensive remarks under her breath about "our work," threatening to expose me as a fraud, to reveal to the world what we both knew to be a fact, she said, that I was nothing without her, that her invisible signature was on every page I'd ever written. From my desk, sitting back in my contoured chair, my eyes closed, my head thrown back, I listened to her, inhaling a fraction of the blanket of smoke she emitted, smelling the butts in the ashtray and in the wastebasket beside the cloth chair where she sat. I was hoping for a moment of peace from her harangue, a moment free of bitterness, and I imagined smoke rushing out of her mouth as if a fire smoldered inside her. When Gail paused to suck on what was left of her cigarette, I leaned forward and rested my hands on the scattered pages of the all-but-finished manuscript, sighing at her and at it, fearing that no more than ten days' work and fretting were left on the book. I was at a point where I felt I had nothing left to give it, though I still wanted to read the damn thing over and over, and the thought of reaching this point of helplessness, when I could do nothing more for the poor dumb bastard and I was at its mercy and it no longer at mine, made me sweat, made my head ache. And it was in this context that Gail decided to make things worse, to do her temperamental, vengeful routine. As I looked at her she took a long puff, squinting.

"So you don't want to talk about me and my problems," she said. "You want to talk about the book, about you, in other words. Or what you think is you."

She couldn't stand the sight of me and her nose looked as if a stench had invaded it. She mashed out her cigarette.

"It is me, Gail."

"Do you think you can do what I do?"

"Probably not as well."

"That's why you keep me in here till we're both depleted and fed up with each other. We sit together through every word and every sentence for three years, not to mention the other four books, and then you get the credit."

"You want me to put footnotes all through the text? I am indebted to my wife, Gail, for her contributions to the arguments between husband and wife, for contributing to the ideas expressed in this or that chapter, for urging me to cut certain passages and scenes, for assisting in the choice of detail throughout and suggesting that I use the following list of words. It's ridiculous, Gail. You know the work is more mine than yours. And you're here because you want to be. I'm not forcing you."

"The books are not just yours and you can see how well you write them without me. I've had it, Brent. It's been going on too long and I can't take it anymore, it's eating me up. Everything that starts out as me turns into you."

"I don't think it's what you want, Gail."

What she said worried me. Gail had dragged us both through her fits and grievances so many times before that the subject nauseated me. For years she'd been grinding out cigarettes in her ashtray as if she were twisting them into my face, but she had not said she was never helping me again. I sometimes felt she was on the verge of saying it, but I sensed that she restrained herself, thinking better of it and letting the impulse pass. Gail was a failed writer and there were satisfactions for her in my work. She'd studied writing in school, had written numerous short stories over a period of years, but was never satisfied with any of them. Both her output and confidence gradually dwindled and her creative energies were rerouted and joined with mine. The choice was hers, and I think she made the right choice.

But seeing her look wronged, listening to the pain in her voice, watching the billows of smoke drift around the room, I almost wished she would skulk out the door and let me breathe some fresh air and stop diverting me from my novel. We'd been in the room since seven in the morning, starting work, as we normally did, before our son and daughter left for school. Any minute they'd be home and the door to the study would be closed to block out the noise, which would add to our sense of nearness and wall in all of the smoke. Battle and Whirl were seventeen and sixteen at the time so they were old enough that they didn't create a riot when they walked through the front door. But they had their share of distracting habits—the televisions in their rooms, the music they listened to, the phone calls, the chatter and parading up and down the hallway. So the door had to be closed to get any work done.

"Is this one of those times when you want me to get out?" Gail asked, sitting up on the edge of her chair. Maybe she'd seen me make a face or bat away a gust of smoke, I don't know. "You wring me out like a sponge, then tell me to beat it. Is that what you have in mind, a little Gail-free silence?"

"I just want to work, Gail."

"All we ever do is work, Brent. I don't know what else to do with it, I can't think of one thing I'd change, and I'm sick of answering your questions and talking you out of your doubts. I'm sick of your voice and of being some nameless employee."

"Take a break then, Gail, goddamn it. In the frame of mind

you're in I couldn't trust what you said anyway. Your brain's all fogged up with grudges and meanness, and I don't want you using this book to get even with me."

"What does that mean? You don't trust me?"

"I know you're bitter."

"After all the time and work I've put in, you're suspicious of me."

"You hold back sometimes. I can feel it. You have ideas but you keep them to yourself. Maybe you're not always aware of it. Maybe you are."

"What about what I do say?"

"What about it?"

"Do I lie? Do I lead you in the wrong direction, or try to?"

"I don't know. You tell me."

"You drive me out of my mind. I can't stand it."

"I'm not sure what you think about the hotel scene."

"I've told you twenty times what I think."

I let out a little snort of doubt before I could stop myself. That snort, so slight that anyone standing ten feet away would probably not have heard it, burned Gail up. The air was suddenly charged, and at that moment, just as Gail was about to explode, the front door opened and Battle and Whirl walked in from school. I got up, dodging toppled piles of manuscript pages, opened books, closed books, Gail's feet, which she made no effort to remove from my path, and shut the door to the room quickly but without a sound.

"Not only are you a paranoid liar and a fraud," Gail said, "you won't even say hello to your children or let them have a look at you."

As Gail talked I paced, struggling to focus on the hotel scene, paper crunching underfoot. Battle and Whirl passed through the hallway to their rooms and they did not say hello to us over their mother's voice on the way. We did not exist for them yet, not until we emerged. Their doors closed and soon I heard the muffled sound of voices and music.

"How you could sit there and say you don't know what I think about the hotel scene is beyond me, after we've eviscerated it time and again," she said, the end of her latest cigarette glowing as she lit up and inhaled. "We've spent more time on that part than anything else, and as I'm sure you remember, it was my idea to put it in the book in the first place."

"I remember." I stopped pacing and stood in front of her. "But you didn't make it up."

"I know, Brent, but it is the most important scene in the book, and the scene you were missing for such a long time."

"I know it is."

"You still don't know if he should throw her out the window."

"I didn't throw you out."

"You probably wanted to but were worried it would hurt your career. It would have hurt your reputation and you would have had to write your fabulous books without me, something you wouldn't have been able to do. And I bet the real reason you're worried about the scene is that I suggested it. You're afraid I've talked you into a bad idea and that I'm laughing behind your back at the thought that everyone who reads the book will hate it and that you'll be branded as a latent wife killer and woman hater."

"So you won't tell me then."

Gail threw up her hands. "I've told you," she insisted.

Maybe she was right, I thought. I was asking for her opinion but I wouldn't believe whatever she told me. Even if she said it was a bad scene I would wonder if she was contriving to get me to take out the best part of the book, or at least to confuse and upset me.

"OK," I said. "You're right." But I still wished I could hear her answer, the truthful one, that is.

"I'm right? You don't believe me then, you don't trust me."

I felt trapped. I didn't want to look at her or answer her. I sat on the edge of my desk, my back halfway to her.

"Sounds like I picked a good day to quit this job," she said. "Your ingratitude staggers me."

"Can we please change the subject, Gail? Can we get off all this flesh rending and do some work?"

"Oh sure, Brent, if you say to change the subject we will. I'll just forget all about what we were saying so you can get some work done."

"Just save it. I'm not saying forget about it."

"But the book is finished and I am finished."

"The book is not quite finished."

"I think it is. I know I am."

"Please, Gail."

"You're just worried because you don't want to let it go," she told me. "And you don't want to let me go because you don't care about anything but your work."

"You won't be happy doing your own work. You never were before."

"I'm not happy now. It's not worth it to me. Remember, in the hotel room he throws her from the window and then says she jumped."

"You're saying I'm throwing you out, but I'm asking you to stay."

"In your way you're throwing me."

"You're jumping."

"I think you wanted to throw me out that day and that later you fantasized about picking me up and pitching me through the window. You might have even dreamed about it, watching me tumble through the air and then thud on the pavement."

"I did want to throw you out, but I stopped."

"You hadn't figured out how to get away with it."

I didn't answer and I resented the pleasure she took in taunting me. There was a caustic smile in the corner of her mouth, and watching her lips turn I imagined her sailing out the window. I imagined grunting with the effort of heaving her out and hanging my head out into the open air, falling to my knees when I saw her laugh at me on the way down.

Gail stubbed out her cigarette, then stood and moved to my desk. She pulled open the drawer that held my gun and I jumped to my feet. I saw her reach for the gun and shift its grip into her hand. I imagined Gail shooting me through the head, splattering my brains all over the walls, standing over me while I spurted blood and twitched. But instead she held the gun up in her face, the barrel pointed at the ceiling, her finger on the trigger. She went back to her chair and sat, still with the gun held up. Then she turned it around and looked down the barrel.

"Stop it, Gail."

I was getting mad. She was threatening me, or that was the way

I took it, and I didn't know if this was a prank or if her face would turn serious and cold and she would pull the trigger.

"You'd nag me to help you, Brent," she began, lowering the gun to her lap. "I'd have to keep saying no to you, and I'd miss it and sooner or later the whole damn thing could start over. I could be in here working anonymously for your benefit. But not with this," she said, gesturing with the gun. "I'd be safe from you and you'd never put out another book, or not another good one. People might start to wonder what became of your talent since your wife died."

"It's my work," I shouted and moved toward her.

"I have an impact on what happens in here. You're afraid for your work right now, aren't you?"

"More than anything I'm angry," I said, my face near hers.

She put her hand over my nose and mouth and pushed me away. I hated Gail at that moment. She stood and came at me, the gun cradled against her chest.

"You're frustrated and afraid, Brent, because you know I'm right."

I heard footsteps in the hall.

"You all right in there, Mama?" Battle asked.

"Just great," Gail answered.

"You want me to wait here?"

"Go back to your room, Oedipus," I told him, "unless you can find it in your heart to come to my aid."

"We're just killing each other," Gail said.

His footsteps moved away and we heard him muttering to himself.

"You don't have to put the Oedipus stigma on him just because he sees what a bloodless shit you are and wants to protect me."

"And I know how you've worked to convince him that I'm a nice guy."

"He can see what you are for himself. He doesn't need to hear it from me."

"He sees me through your eyes."

"I wish you did. But we were talking about your fear."

"I was talking about my anger."

"Which grew out of your fear."

"Which grew out of being harassed by you."

"Naturally you're the victim since the earth revolves around you."

"I didn't start all this."

"You're the cause of it. That means you started it. You just don't see it that way."

She was still right on me, breathing her smoke-scented hot air up my nose, and I was tired of listening to her and having my gun between us. I grabbed the gun with one hand and with the other I nudged her away to give myself room. She stumbled sideways, still holding the gun, and braced herself against the desk to keep from going down. She regained her footing and lunged back at me. I hit her with my open hand and she released her grip, falling backwards. She landed on her butt, groaning, and swayed as she tried to get to her feet. She sank back to the floor, her legs spread, and put her hand to her nose, which bled. The door swung open and Battle rushed in, his eyes going to her.

"I heard the pop," he said, dropping to his knee. He held Gail's head and tilted it back. The blood ran between her fingers and dripped down her chin. He glanced up and saw what I was holding.

"Did you hit her with that?"

"No."

I held up my empty hand and then dropped it at my side. I felt numb watching the blood run out of Gail. I put the gun on the desktop and drifted to the bathroom off the study for a towel. I came back with the towel and flipped it down to Battle, who pressed it to Gail's nose. Whirl was in the doorway, her open mouth covered with her hand.

"How did it feel?" Battle asked before looking up, and at first I wasn't sure if he was asking me or Gail.

"I don't know," I said.

Gail stirred, getting her feet under her and putting her weight against Battle.

"Get me out of here," she said through the towel.

He helped her up, his eyes on me. He looked at the gun, which lay amid the pages of *Deep Wilderness,* and then he turned with Gail and led her out. Whirl backed up and walked away, and Battle closed the door.

BATTLE

Reading the twentieth-anniversary edition of my mother and father's celebrated fifth novel, *Deep Wilderness*, has stirred up waves of memories from the days when the novel was being written, the days before it was begun and stretching on into the years that followed, until my mother's death and beyond. It is mainly of the circumstances surrounding her death and of my parents' miserable lives together that I want to write. Long ago I gave up the idea of living with these memories. I do not live with them but against them, and though there is no hope of banishing these pieces of family history from my mind, I want to tell the story for my mother's sake, so that her death will be put in some kind of context and her life will not recede into an underserved oblivion.

In a sense my mother and father both died the day she decided not to work with him anymore, which was just as they were completing *Deep Wilderness*. As anyone who has followed the Great Man's career knows, his work reached its height with *DW*, his most complex work, with its shifting viewpoints and narrative dislocations, and since then it has diminished in quantity while plummeting in quality. Some critics have gone so far as to ask if the same person wrote the last two novels, both slender and disappointing, as wrote *DW* and the four novels before it. The truth is that the same people did not write them, only he did. My father is a has-been, as even he realizes, and he became one the day my mother quit and left him to write his books himself. Why I would decide to become a writer after growing up in that house I'll never know. I can still hear the study door closing when my sister Whirl and I came home from school. I can hear their voices, usually my mother's, coming from behind it, the house full of her cigarette smoke. I used to wonder how they could breathe in there with all that smoke and how they could work for so long with each other in that room. Sometimes when he'd had enough of her and her smoke he would throw her out, but other times she would walk out herself, telling him that she couldn't think and she needed a rest. He could stay in there forever if he wanted to, but she was going to talk to her children, to find out what life was like outside the room. He would call after her that they were almost through for the day. "Just another hour, Gail, just till the end of the paragraph, damn you." Some afternoons when we came in from school she'd be stretched out on the sofa in the den, her feet up, an ashtray in her lap and a cigarette in her mouth, her hand still holding it. She would look drained and dazed when she looked up at us. She might whisper a curse in the direction of our father because he'd banished her or she might look at us in silence. We could see her anger, her resentment of him. She couldn't hide it, it was part of her. And going down the hallway to our rooms we would pass the closed door where the Great Man was at work, pounding his typewriter or chasing words and images through his mind.

Whenever he threw her out, Mother cooked dinner, and we ate around seven, when the Great Man came out of his room. He would be worn out, and his clothes, which he changed every four or five days, would often smell of dried sweat. Our dinners were awkward. He seldom spoke and preferred not to talk about the work, preferred to keep it out of his mind until the next morning. He breathed heavily through his mouth, rubbed his face and at times let out a lengthy yawn. He would look up at Whirl and me, at a loss for words. When Mother stayed in the room till seven we would usually eat takeout food. We ate quietly and fast, not wanting to prolong our discomfort.

After dinner they drank, he more than she did, but both of them steadily pouring it in, becoming increasingly relaxed, he sitting in his chair with a book most of the time, his reading lamp hanging over his shoulder, Mother either reading or staring at nothing or into herself, contemplating her life, I supposed. If Whirl and I wanted to watch TV, we did it in our rooms and Mother occasionally would watch with us. But both Whirl and I read. We read other people's books and we read the books with our father's name on them, hoping to bring him nearer, especially Whirl, who read them again and again. But reading them was confusing since we often wondered if what we read belonged to him or to our mother, or both of them. We didn't ask, because the subject was taboo.

After Mother left him alone inside his room, sealed behind his door, she began her own work again. While the Great Man put in his usual long hours in his study, Mother worked all day at the kitchen table. She filled up pads with drafts of stories, sometimes ten or twelve versions of each one, notes covering the margins, lines written between lines, pages ripped out and wadded into tiny yellow balls. She squeezed these tiny balls in her hands as she hunched over the table and read the drafts. When I passed through the kitchen I'd ask her how it was going. Usually she shook her head or looked at me with humility and said nothing.

On and on she went. When she'd decided she could do nothing more with a story she'd send it out. Form rejections frequently came back. Sometimes an editor took the trouble to explain why he or she found a story disagreeable, or why one or all of the characters did not engage the reader's interest. But as hard as they both worked, neither of them was succeeding alone. It was obvious from the start and it did not change.

They still slept in the same room and the same bed. Whirl and I waited for their sleeping arrangement to change but it never did. We heard them fighting in their bedroom after they'd closed their door for the night, lashing each other with bitter words on into the night, even after their lights were out and they lay together, side by side.

Mother kept writing for four years before she gave it up. Whirl and I were away at college by then and we avoided going home, though we did return for visits occasionally. It was depressing to go back and see them—our father in decline, our mother failing, a look of emptiness and desperation in their eyes. But I talked to Mother regularly on the phone and it was one night when I called that she broke down and told me she'd quit, she couldn't do it on her own, she was lost. I could tell she'd had quite a bit to drink and I knew from my trips home that she was drinking more than she used to, almost as much as the Great Man, who was also pouring down more than ever. She had no idea what to do with herself, she said, no idea where to go from where she was, but she was determined not to go into that room with him again. And he was as bad off as she was, she went on, her voice perking up all of a sudden. He was in the habit of going by himself to the movies in the afternoon rather than facing his deficiencies on the page. He'd get in an uproar if he found out she'd told me. He'd warned her to keep quiet about it, not to tell anyone, particularly me or Whirl. He was humiliated and wore sunglasses when he snuck out of the house.

He probably looked over his shoulder and in the rearview mirror all the way to the theater and wouldn't even have gone unless it was dark in the movie. "Mr. Incognito," she told me, laughing, "as if anyone on earth would care, as if anyone would be watching him." She said that he even took the newspaper into his study when he worked and spread it out on his desk and read it. She'd stood outside the closed door and listened to the paper rustling. "He won't give in and neither will I," she said. "His reputation is at stake and he will never let me have the credit I'm due. And if he's prepared to let me stew and wither, I'm ready to let him do the same."

For a year after finishing *Deep Wilderness* my father claimed that he was spent from the effort he'd put into the novel, that he needed time to replenish his energy and was merely in a slump. But the slump endured. He could not produce work he was satisfied with, and whenever I went home I could see his loss of faith in himself. His face was shrunken and hollow and his posture and bearing had changed. His voice and eyes, his gestures and movements carried no force. His mind wandered as he sat in his chair in the den holding his drink. The Great Man's reading habits also changed. He could hardly bear the sight of good work because his recent efforts did not measure up. He still felt a desire to read, so he indulged, but not as consistently or as fondly as he had. Often, instead of reading, he watched thrillers or mysteries on television to kill time in the evenings, cursing at the dialogue, talking back to the characters on the screen when their behavior seemed absurd to him. Still, he went on watching, slumped and inert in his chair, dissatisfied but involved, critical yet tolerant.

And the longer Mother went without helping him the more he hated and feared her. The longer the Great Man went without writing anything worthwhile, the more persuasive her case would be if she exposed him. She taunted him with his failures and ridiculed him. They bickered and drank, their arguments escalating into furious rows, into an engulfing bitterness that lasted for days.

It was not until just days before her death, when Whirl and I were both in graduate school, that Mother ever said anything to me about leaving him. She'd been thinking the idea over for years, she said, at first in the back of her mind, dreading and resisting it, and then more consciously, her thoughts slowly migrating to the front of her mind until she could think of little else. She hated being in the same house with him and seeing him dwindle into nothingness, and she was weary of listening to herself rave on about what a thorough dog he was. She didn't love him, didn't respect him, and she was beginning to realize that she was through with him. She'd shouted during an argument a few nights before that she was getting out if he wouldn't and she wasn't going to waste what was left of her life with him. He'd yelled that she was staying and pleaded with her when she ignored him. He'd held her, crying, and wouldn't let her go until she said she would stay. She'd been afraid and had given in.

She was still weak, she told me. She knew she wanted to end her old life, but an abyss awaited her. Her reality was with him, and she had known no other for twenty-five years. She said she intended to reveal that she'd collaborated with him, to claim that he had defrauded the public, that she was entitled to a share of royalties from all the books he'd published, and she would not rest until she had seen justice. And he sensed that the end was coming and feared that she would end her silence, and he could not sleep. His body was coated with a glaze of sweat, she said, which was partly made up of the vodka oozing from his pores. An aura of defeat hung over him, but he also went into periods of desperate anger that alarmed her.

This was our final conversation, and whenever I think of Mother's death, which is often, I remember what she said, searching her words for nuances and clues. When the Great Man phoned me with the news that he'd found her dead, hanging from the scaffolding of the garage door, my first thought as I listened to him choke out the words was that he'd killed her. I imagined his glaze of sweat, his anger.

"Is she quiet?" I asked him.

"Quiet?"

"What happened?"

"She was drunk, Battle. Very drunk. You know how unhappy she'd been."

"Did she pass out?"

"No, she didn't just pass out. Do you understand what I'm saying?"

"When did you find her?"

"This morning after I got up."

"Didn't you notice that she wasn't in bed?"

"Yeah, I noticed, but I did sleep pretty well. Maybe, to tell you the truth, because she wasn't lying there berating me half the night, or tossing and turning or making just enough noise to keep me awake. Anyway, I thought she'd gotten up to go in the other room and stare into space. She'd been doing that. And maybe I was right, I don't know. She could have stared into space, drinking."

"Did she leave a message?"

"No. I guess killing herself was a message to me, though. I can't deny it to you, Battle."

I made the seven hour drive home, in a rage most of the way, talking out loud to him, visualizing a confrontation and a fight. But as I neared the house I began to question my suspicions, to tell myself that I was overlooking all the reasons my mother had to kill herself. There was nothing to confront him with, not as far as I knew.

And when I saw him coming toward me in utter agony as I walked through the front door, when I felt his arms tighten around me, I cried with him when he said: "I guess I'm the reason she did it. I guess I ruined her life."

Whirl arrived two hours after I did. She was halfway gone from the time she walked in, but when she saw him she went to pieces. He squeezed her, rocking her in his arms, and kissed her cheeks. I hugged her while he put his hands on our backs.

We sat in the den for I don't know how long, not saying much, not having much eye contact, my father rubbing his forehead and looking bewildered. Then we went through the door to the garage, which was connected to the house, and he pointed up at the place where he'd found her hanging. Against the wall, he showed us, was the stool she'd stood on. We stared at the place and walked around it. Whirl, looking ill, hurried back in the house. He and I watched her go through the door and then my eyes caught his.

"I'm glad you're both here," he said. And then: "I loved your mother."

At the sparsely attended funeral the next day he was the embodiment of grief. A thick drizzle fell nonstop and his eyes never moved from the coffin or the grave. He held me and Whirl at his sides and he blubbered and moaned, his legs sinking under his weight, his body as soft as the water that gradually soaked our clothes and dripped down our faces with our tears. "She was part of me," he said to us as the first shovelful of dirt fell on her.

When I look back at those two days I see my father's sentiment as no more than an act meant to charm me and Whirl, a spell to divert our attention from the cause of our mother's death. I had never seen him cry before and had never heard him say that he loved my mother.

It was just after the funeral that I found myself distrusting the feelings he'd shown. I could think of arguments to make against my distrust. He'd never suffered the death of a spouse before, so why should it seem strange that he would show feelings that seemed different to me? Why should I expect him to behave in a familiar way in an unfamiliar situation, a situation in which the one closest to him in the world had died? But I was not convinced, and I saw his apparent grief as a performance too exaggerated to be believed.

Whirl and I drove back to school the following day and when we left he already appeared within himself again, unhappy in a resentful way, but under control, subduing his usual self-centered disposition, not wanting us to see, I suspected, the same man we were used to seeing. He was ready to be rid of us, I imagined, ready to rip off the mask and shut himself up alone in his study to sit and wonder if there was some way he could be caught, a detail or a loose end that could arouse the suspicion of some zealous detective. Walking out the door I stared straight into his face to see what was there. I caught him, I believe, with his guard down, with no time to throw up his edifice of sorrow. He shrank, just noticeably, and I saw his Adam's apple bob as he swallowed. His face colored and quickly he patted me on the shoulder and said, "We'll never forget her, Battle, will we?" "No," I said. He looked at Whirl and she hugged him. She and I made our way to our cars and we waved at him as we pulled away. Looking back at him in my rearview mirror I saw him turn in our direction, frowning.

I lay awake that night, unable to close my eyes. I kept seeing him carry Mother out to the garage after she'd passed out from drinking, putting the rope around her neck and hoisting her into the air. I kept thinking of the way he'd seemed from the time

Whirl and I got home until the time we'd left, the words he'd said, the look of his eyes and face. I remembered Mother telling me that she was still weak, that the only reality she knew was with him, and I tried to picture her on her own with nothing to sustain her but a vendetta against her future ex-husband. I wondered if she'd experienced a moment of extreme panic, of cowardice.

I wanted to talk to him about her and knew I couldn't rest until I had. It was after midnight and I could have been waking him from a deep sleep, but I called him anyway. He picked it up after the second ring.

"Yes."

"It's Battle."

"I figured," he said.

"Were you asleep?"

"Yes, I was. I hope you won't hold that against me, but I'm done in. When I hit the bed I couldn't keep my eyes open."

"I'm just the opposite."

"So be it then."

"Are you surprised she did it? I can't imagine her putting a rope around her neck. I know there are reasons she could have done it, but it doesn't seem real to me."

"She did do it, Battle. And I guess she had her reasons. Even though we weren't happy with each other the most fulfilling moments in her life happened right here in this house. She saw you and Whirl grow up here and there was the work we did. But all of that was over. I would have welcomed her back myself because I valued what she did. But she didn't want to work with me anymore, our marriage was a wreck, and to her it may have seemed that her life was at a total dead end. Does that make sense to you?"

"I suppose it could add up."

"I'm sure I wonder about it as much as you do, but we only have ideas. We can't say what really happened."

"She may not have known what happened herself."

"That's right," he said, hesitantly, I thought.

"Still, in the book you throw her out the window."

"It wasn't her in the book, Battle. Those were characters."

"They were characters, but some of the things in the book were real. You had a major fight in a hotel room, didn't you?"

"We did, but I never threw your mother out of a window."

"Was it a rough day between you the day she died?"

"They were all rough. Maybe you should let me get some sleep."

"Are you relaxed enough to sleep?"

"Look, I know you loved your mother more than you love me and that you basically sympathize with her and feel contempt for me, but I hope that you will not dedicate yourself the way she did to butting heads and making trouble."

"You're right, I don't like you. And I don't trust you."

"You could have picked a better time to tell me."

"From my point of view there has never been a better time."

"That's not fair to me."

"Maybe it isn't. But I still mean what I said."

"You're as cruel as she was."

"You helped fill her life with suffering and now she's dead and she'll never know a better one."

"She had a better one and gave it up. She gave up everything, but there is nothing we can do about it now."

"There was something you could have done about it," I answered, leaving him speechless.

I hung up.

WHIRL

My brother Battle has a dark bias against our father, and though he may say that he does not know that Brent killed our mother, he acts and thinks as if he does know, despite the fact that there is no evidence to support his conviction. So by saying he doesn't know he is both telling the truth (because he doesn't know) and at the same time he is being a hypocrite (because he thinks he does know). He is unjust to Brent, walks around thinking our father is a murderer, resents him as if he knows it, looks at him as if he knows it, talks as if he knows it. Battle wants to blame someone other than our mother for her death, and our father is a good man for the job because of his obnoxious personality and his insensitivity to his family, especially his wife, who devoted most of her adult life to him while he appreciated her only in the most selfish way.

Battle says I can't get all the way out of the habit of looking up to Brent, and according to him that is the reason I don't see things the way he sees them. I admire my father, it's true, although I admired him more when I was younger, when I saw only that he wrote books and that his work was difficult and required almost all of his time and energy. But slowly I found myself feeling left out, feeling a mounting frustration because of the distance he put between us. I could remember when I was small and he played with me in the yard, chasing me, holding me up high in the air and then kissing my face and smiling. I missed his smile and missed when he held me, which he did again for the first time in years and years after Mother died.

And while Battle accuses me of looking up to Brent, he is the one who became a writer. He is the one who set out to do what Brent did. He has published a book of stories and a novel that have been fairly well received, but they've suffered by comparison with Brent's first two books, as well as the next three, a fact that infuriates Battle. He raves that the Great Man didn't write the books alone and so does not deserve full credit for their existence. He has used a couple of interviews, one in a newspaper, the other in a widely circulated literary review, to downgrade Brent's achievement, to say that he resents being compared with him and that our mother played an essential role in what is thought of as Brent's work. It seems to me that Battle is not only following in Brent's footsteps, but also hoping to surpass him and to fulfill Mother's unrealized dream, walking in her unrealized footsteps, trying to achieve a vicarious wish fulfillment. My brother claims that the only footsteps he is walking in are his own.

Actually Battle has been no more successful as a family man than Brent was. He was married to a painter who wanted as much time for her work as he wanted for his and the result was that when they weren't fighting about being broke or who would tend to the baby or whose work was more important, they were busy working, ignoring Alice and Rex, their children, who were unhappy and have grown more and more troubled. They are now six and eight years old and are both under psychiatric care and both have problems dealing with other children and everyone else.

They bite people, spit on them and are verbally hostile. They have developed physical ailments such as eczema, asthma, and frequent cold sores. Battle began drinking heavily while he was married, and so did his wife, which made everything worse, and eventually the family situation became unbearable and they split up. Battle has nothing good to say about his ex-wife but complains that she badmouths him whenever she gets half a chance. He avoids his children and feels uncomfortable whenever he sees them, and they are obviously not at ease around their father. They are relieved to get away from him and he is relieved to return them to their mother. He fears that for the rest of his life there will be trouble with one of them or both of them, one problem, one nuisance after another. But as bad a father as my brother was and is, he shows no restraint in commenting on what a bad father Brent was and how he cheated every one of us out of a share of happiness that could have been ours. And his failures as a husband have not tempered his rage toward Brent for his treatment of our mother. Battle has grown to be strangely like the person he thinks the least of in the world, as if he wanted to become that very person. I can't say why. Maybe it is his way of trying to become close to him.

Battle and I have differences on the subject of our father, but I do see Brent's failings and I do not doubt that he may have killed our mother and, like Battle, I feel enraged when I think of it, just as if I knew what happened. I have spent days and nights without sleep thinking he is guilty and hating him for it and wanting him to pay. I despise him for the way he used Mother and wish she had left him, and it sickens me to think of the way her life ended. Even if she slipped the rope over her head and tightened it around her neck herself, I believe he is partly responsible for it, and I grieve for her and suffer in the face of my memories of her. But I do not know that he killed her and I do not want to think he killed her and I am afraid that he did.

But maybe Brent is a victim of Mother's. Maybe she killed herself as an act of revenge against him, and if she did, her revenge has been more successful than she may ever have thought it would be. Battle believes that Brent murdered her, and I am suspicious of him. Maybe Mother foresaw how we would react and purposely said things to Battle that would later lead him to think that Brent killed her. Or maybe there was no premeditation by her of any kind. Maybe she couldn't take it anymore and ended it. I waver from one point of view to another. He is a killer, he is not a killer. She is a suicide, she is not a suicide. Battle does not know what happened, I am afraid he is right about what happened. I suspect my father, I am being unfair to my father. I will probably never know who or what finished my mother, never know if the legacy of her death was left by her or by him. And I want the subject out of my mind and I cannot get it out of my mind.

BATTLE

The Great Man and no one else wrote the three chapters before this one, chapters in which he tells the story of himself and our family, and without actually confessing, the story of how he could have killed his wife. And though he is the person behind the narrative he does not make himself seem as sympathetic as he could have in any of the chapters, not even in the one in his own name. Not only could he have chosen to tell the story a different way, he could have chosen not to write it at all. I have wondered what he hopes to gain by publishing this manuscript and why he has offered to allow me to contribute to it without fear of having him edit what I write or remove it. Why should he suddenly be interested in using his clout to print my viewpoint in a work that is basically his? Could this man, who before has always acted according to self-interest, be trying to tell us something? My father has the look of a haunted man, and when I ask him about this manuscript he is all furtiveness and reticence and will offer me no clue about why he would do something that is so unlike him and about what has caused him to change. The only answer I have been able to come up with is guilt, a guilt that will not release him. If Mother had killed herself I believe he would have found some way out in his mind, a trapdoor to slip through that would have freed him from a sense of blame. He could have attributed her death to her weaknesses as a person, her failure to deal with her shortcomings as a writer, her envy of him. Even if he believed she killed herself out of a desire for revenge against him, or possibly a displaced desire to kill him, he could still tell himself it was her decision to do what she did and her hand that did it. But he has found no trapdoor for himself, which says to me that there is none, that the reason she is dead is plain to him.

I am encouraged by his apparent desire to expose himself but wish that he'd revealed more. Also, I do object to the description of me in his chapter in Whirl's name. I am not as much like my father as he seems to want to believe. My ex-wife is alive, just to name one big difference, and her work does not appear under my name. And while I admit feeling awkward with my children I look forward to seeing them and feel a sense of loss whenever they leave and go back to Catherine. I don't think it's unfair to say that the Great Man has an ax to grind against me and that what he has written should be read with that in mind. My father has told me he can think of no better name for the present manuscript than *Deep Wilderness*, a repetition that could be a sign of his guilt turning him toward his life in the past. But the story he has told probably will not ease his conscience, nor will naming it after the only novel he ever wrote in which the major character kills his wife.

BRENT

What I have to say is simple: I wrote none of the previous chapters. Battle wrote them, which explains why they are all so slanted against me. Anyone who is both gullible and suspicious enough to doubt what I am saying should pause and ask himself whether I would ask Battle to add a chapter to a manuscript I wrote. And if I felt the need to confess I would just confess rather than using other people's voices to dance around it. It irks me to involve myself in Battle's account, but he has offered me the opportunity to add a chapter in my own words and I have little choice but to defend myself. Whirl told me that she refuses "to say anything about who wrote what." She wants to stay completely out of it, doesn't want to associate herself with the family's bickering, and I understand that and don't blame her. But where does that leave me? Battle sees no problem with letting me have my say. He said he doubted anyone would be persuaded that my hands are clean anyway and that my chapter would add dimension and texture to his work. I told him he was using me and my words for his own ends. He said I'd done exactly the same thing to Gail, and he sounded just like her when he said it.

And it bothers me that he has given this work the same title as my best book, *Deep Wilderness*. I take this choice as a further way of ridiculing me.

I prefer not to say more.

BATTLE

Though my father seems unable to silence the voice of his guilt, he fears suffering the consequences, and so he hides behind other people's voices and then ascribes them to me and stops short of making an overt confession.

GAIL

Brent and I do other things, attend our writing workshop and classes, teach our undergraduate students, but our real life is at the kitchen table in our small apartment where we work on the novel together. And the work we do is better than anything we did alone. There is a feeling of excitement, a sense of accomplishment that we never had before. After a night at the table we go to bed and usually make love and then go right to sleep, utterly exhausted. Brent is talented, industrious, and ruthless about his work, all of which attracts me. I am not as talented as he is, but I am able to give him what he needs. From me he gets a sense of place, richer dialogue, more vivid detail, and a source of control for his chronic overwriting. But I realize that I cannot do what he does, cannot imagine as deeply as he imagines, create the situations or conflicts that he comes up with. Yet with his help I am able to fill in blank areas, holes in the drama that escape him and that formerly he had to gloss over, with skill, admittedly, but the holes did show.

We will be finished with school in a month and we have talked about marriage and plan to go through with it soon after we have our degrees. We will then complete the novel, which Brent had started work on several months before we got together. My stories are in the background now, but after the manuscript is completed and on its way I intend to focus on them again. Brent doesn't seem to worry about my stories and how little time I spend on them. He is self-absorbed and anyone can see that he is arrogant, but I feel lucky that he has let me through the wall around him into his life. What we are doing is of value to both of us. There is a glue, we share an ambition, and no one else gives him what I give him.

But something happened that makes me think. One day about a week ago I noticed that Brent looked distant and bothered. He was quiet and didn't want to talk about it with me, but later, while we were sitting at the table working, tearing apart some scene or some sentence, pages of manuscript all around us, the air clouded with smoke from my cigarettes, I sensed that he felt crowded by me, annoyed that I was there. His concentration had left the manuscript and had turned toward me. He seemed to be suffocating on my smoke and was wincing and sighing and rubbing his face. I watched him and waited, afraid of what he would say. He looked in my eyes and said he wanted to work by himself for a while, to have some silence and be on his own. He asked me to go in the bedroom and work on my own stories or to go out somewhere and occupy myself. He was afraid too, I could see, and we were both uncomfortable, but he did not want me sitting at that table, my mind mingling with his. Without a word I left the apartment and started walking, seeing nothing, my mind racing over the message he had sent me. I knew he'd felt the same way at times before and had held it in or stolen a few hours alone with the manuscript at the library. But he had never sent me away or made me feel that he was putting distance between us that separated me from a work I'd felt myself a part of. In his annoyance, in the tone of his words, he'd made me feel used and unwanted.

I went into a movie and sat there without looking at it, in turmoil and fear, not knowing what to expect when I went back, irritated by the laughter of the people around me, which sounded insipid and silly. I kept thinking of Brent alone at the table, working. I was furious, and I wanted to go back to him and have it be over.

After the movie I left the theater and wandered, and then I went to our apartment. When I walked in he looked at me at once and got up from the table as I looked back at him. He took a step or two in my direction, his pen still in his hand. I saw that he wanted me there and I walked toward the table, toward him, still angry, but wanting to make it better and not worse. He seemed worried that I was upset, but did not seem sorry and said nothing. My eyes moved to the wadded yellow pages on the tabletop, to the hand-written manuscript. I saw that he was in exactly the same place where we'd left off and I admit I was glad to see it. I glanced back at him and noticed his eyes leaving the same page of the manuscript, and he shrugged at me and smiled. We held each other, both of us still, both of us uneasy. And I asked myself when he would want me to leave him alone again and what would happen when he did and how things, in time, would change between us.